I dedicate this book to my big brothers, Cornelius and Rodney. You have always been there to spoil me, help me, support me, and get me out of trouble when I was a child doing childlike things. I also dedicate this book to my baby sister, Star, affectionately known as Cookie. You are my legacy—remember to be better than I. I love you all!

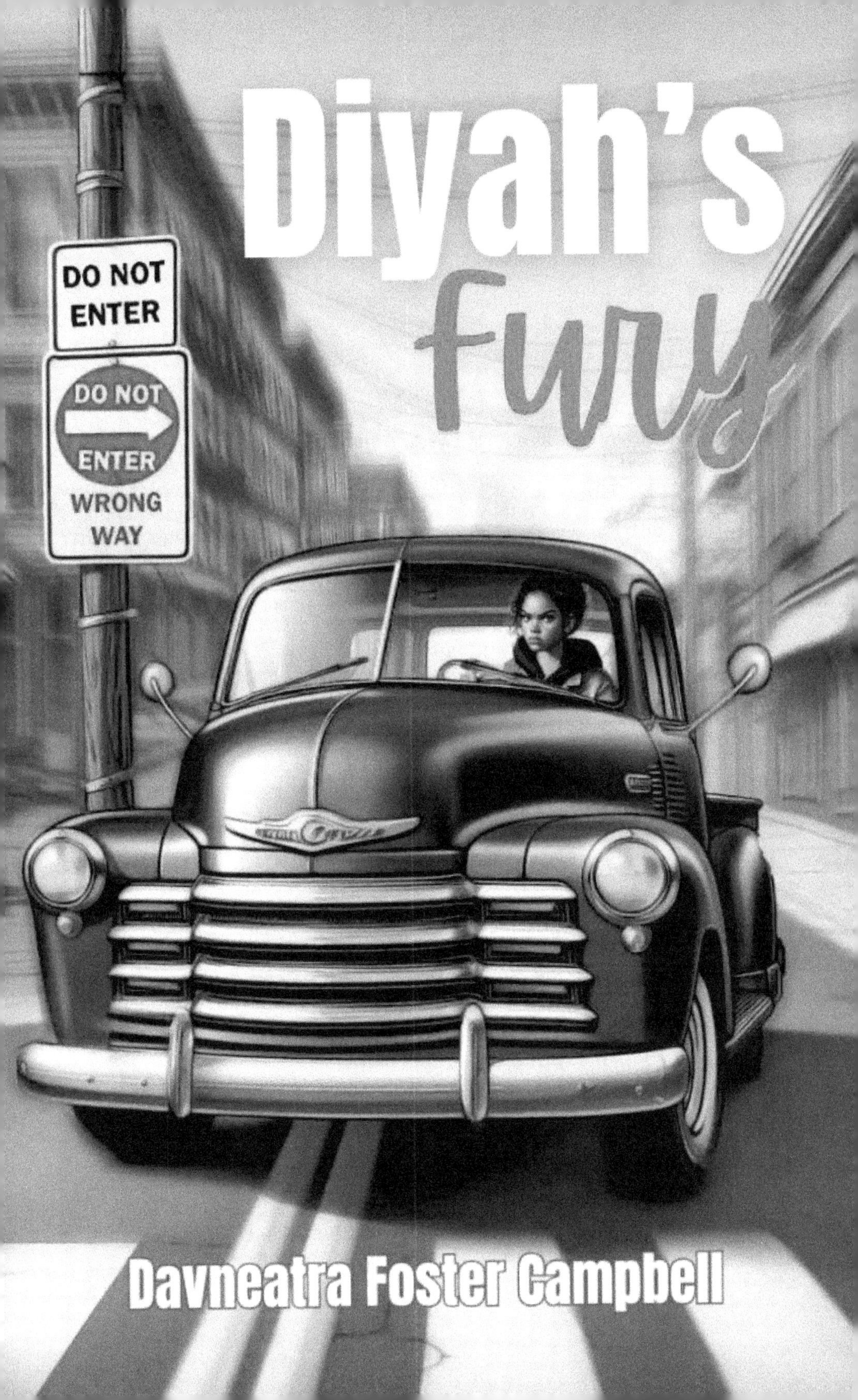
Diyah's
Fury
DO NOT
ENTER
DO NOT
ENTER
WRONG
WAY
Davneatra Foster Campbell

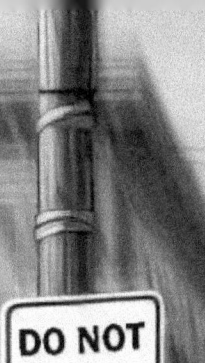

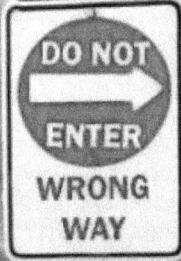

Published by Purposely Booked Publishing
Raleigh, North Carolina

First Edition, 2025
Interior and cover design by Purposely Booked Publishing

Scripture References
The King James Version is in the public domain. Copy and distribute freely.

THE HOLY BIBLE, NEW INTERNATIONAL VERSION®, NIV® Copyright © 1973, 1978, 1984, 2011 by Biblica, Inc.® Used by permission. All rights reserved worldwide.

Scripture quotations marked MSG are taken from THE MESSAGE. Copyright © 1993, 2002, 2018 by Eugene H. Peterson. Used by permission of NavPress. All rights reserved. Represented by Tyndale House Publishers, a Division of Tyndale House Ministries.

ISBN: 979-8-9986404-7-6 (Paperback)
Library of Congress Control Number: 2025923349

Printed in the United States of America.

Disclaimer:
This is a work of fiction. Names, characters, places, and incidents are either the product of the author's imagination or used fictitiously. Any resemblance to actual persons, living or dead, or actual events is purely coincidental.

Table of Contents

Prologue: 7

Chapter 1:
The Aftermath of Pride 9

Chapter 2:
Trigger Warning 13

Chapter 3:
The Discovery.. 19

Chapter 4:
Daddy's Lil' Girl.. 25

Chapter 5:
Draw the Veil 33

Chapter 6:
Sisterly Love... 39

Chapter 7:
Bosom of Fools 47

Chapter 8:
A Daughter Never Outgrows the Heart 55

Chapter 9:
In Everything Give Thanks – Part 1 65

Chapter 10:
In Everything Give Thanks – Part 2 71

Chapter 11:
Attorney Client Privilege 85

Chapter 12:
Mercy.. 89

Chapter 13:
Home Sweet Home, Finally................................ 97

Chapter 14:
Capture a Moment..105

Chapter 15:
The Run Away 111

Chapter 16:
Christmas Eve 117

Chapter 17:
Christmas 127

Chapter 18:
It's a Small World 139

Chapter 19:
Case Closed 153

Chapter 20:
Family Reunion 167

Epilogue: 181

Prologue
Six months Previously

Dakota stood there, frozen, fixated on the limp body before them. They looked around, checking to see if anybody was observing this act, but it was hard to see with only the light coming from the moon. Dakota noticed how their own body was shaking uncontrollably. They bent down to check for a pulse. There was a pulse. In that moment, Dakota realized they'd been holding their breath. *Breathe, Dakota*, they thought. They wipe the rain from their forehead. They hadn't planned to do this, and they'd never done anything like this before. They were so consumed by their emotions that they became consumed by rage.

Ten minutes ago, they'd followed this umber-complected older gentleman after his daughter had confronted him, crying on the street. Dakota had watched the two interact. The gentleman apologized repeatedly, but his daughter did not accept his apology. She said he would never change, and he'd disappointed her all her life. She said that he would never be allowed to see her or his grandchildren again. The daughter, who appeared to be in her 40s, got into her dark sedan and sped away, leaving her father there pleading to her taillights. That's when Dakota started to follow him. Before they knew it, they struck him in the head from behind repeatedly with an umbrella.

They heard a sound which brought them back to the present. They noticed the body began to stir and to moan. "I'm so sorry, I'm so sorry," they whisper to the older gentleman. "Please forgive me." Then, Dakota runs off into an alley towards the dark. They needed to disappear into the darkness. They needed to think while they ran. They promised themselves they would never do this again if they could get away with it, but then Dakota realized how good that felt. They rationalized. *He deserved it. It's not like I killed him*, Dakota thought. Then a malicious smile spread across their face as they continued running deeper into the darkness, allowing the darkness to consume them.

Chapter 1
The Aftermath of Pride

Breaking news tonight, Raleigh police are investigating another assault on a father. This has been the third attack this month. X has begun calling the assailant "the FC Attacker". The FC apparently stands for Father Complex. Our WRAL news tracker got this video image from the scene. Authorities are not releasing the names of any of the victims to protect their privacy, but they are stating that all these fathers are African American, dark-complexioned men who are in their '70s. No arrest has been made at this time. The police seemingly have no suspects, but they are assuring the public that this is an ongoing investigation. We will keep you updated as this story unfolds. Also breaking news-

Diyah, pronounced Dee-yah, cuts off her TV. She says out loud to herself, "I wish the FC Attacker would attack my good-for-nothing deadbeat daddy, but he doesn't fit the description." Diyah immediately flashes back to Thanksgiving last year. She learned over Thanksgiving dinner that the man who'd raised her and who had been there all her life, Dawson Jones, was not her biological father. Her mother, Daisy Jones, and Dawson kept this secret from her for 28 years. She learned that she was the reason for their divorce. Despite their divorce, Dawson, the man she thought was her father, had raised her, provided for her, been there for school plays, dance recitals, her prom, taught her how to drive, and was present at every academic accomplishment and graduation. Although he was present, Diyah had felt a void in her life because of how he treated her older sister, Danita, differently from her, and now she knew why. As much as Diyah was angry at her mother and Dawson, she loathed her biological father. He is the one she wished to be attacked by the FC Attacker. She hated to admit it, but Dawson stepped up when her own flesh and blood didn't. Diyah looks at her phone to check the date. She notices her hand is shaking. It was exactly 3 weeks until Thanksgiving this year. It had been almost 12 months since she had any form of communication with her mother or Dawson, and she barely spoke to her older sister these days. She didn't blame her sister for anything, but it was just too painful to talk to her.

She looks at herself in the front-facing camera on her phone and takes note of the reflection. She'd known throughout the years she looked different from her mother, Dawson, and her sister; other people even highlighted her fair complexion, light brown wavy hair, her light brown eyes, her 5'4" height, and the absence of freckles that her mom and sister possessed. Everything about her was a contrast to her family's. Diyah was told that she inherited her looks from another relative, and now she knows that the relative was her biological father. Diyah glances at an unopened envelope lying on her end table. Her mother mailed a letter to her last year after the tragedy of Thanksgiving. She only knew it was a letter because her mom texted her letting her know she was dropping one in the mail. Diyah had not opened any mail from her mom or Dawson, but this envelope haunted her. She stares at it and throws her phone down onto the couch, causing one of her kitty cats to stir.

Diyah continues to reflect. She was also mad at herself because her life had changed so much since that Thanksgiving dinner. Her life now was a downgrade, and it reinforced her depression symptoms and caused a recurring cycle. Up until last year, she was a traveling Registered Nurse. She'd given up her nursing career because she developed severe clinical depression symptoms and panic symptoms, which impaired her functioning. She had even lost her bedside manner with the patients. Presently, Diyah was a bartender at a hole-in-the-wall bar downtown Raleigh on Wilmington Street. Despite her mind being in a constant fog, all she had to remember was how to mix drinks, and that would be a challenge if she worked somewhere else. However, her patrons did not care how well the drinks were mixed as long as they were being served alcohol. Since she'd taken a pay cut from RN to bartender, she had to move into a one-bedroom, one-bath apartment outside of Raleigh and live modestly. She even had to trade in her 2023 Toyota Camry and buy a cash car from her savings, a 1953 green Chevy pickup truck. It wasn't a looker aesthetically on the outside, but the previous owner had completely restored everything underneath the hood before he had a financial crisis, and he sold it to her for a steal. Her savings and the occasional door dashing helped her make ends meet in the present day.

Diyah's apartment wasn't located in the best neighborhood. She lived on the 3rd floor of a brick, low-income housing apartment complex. The moss growing up the side and the spray-painted graffiti made her building easily identifiable when she had deliveries. The inside of her apartment looked better than the outside. Inside her apartment consisted of beige walls throughout, sandhill brown carpet from her living room to bedroom, a one butt kitchen, no seating for dining, a living room only big enough to fit her dark teal faux leather couch, one rustic wooden end table, a cat scratching post, and a litter box in the corner. She had a 32" flatscreen TV she brought from her old place that was mounted on the wall. Her bedroom was big enough for a full-size bed, a dresser with a mirror, a Chester dresser, and another litter box. Diyah's other furniture from her old life was in storage. Diyah's bonded pair of chocolate point Himalayan cats, who were brother and sister, were her only true joy nowadays. Jaylen, the male cat, was now lying on her chest, purring, and seeking some attention since she'd woken him up when she threw her phone, while his sister, Sierra, was laying at her feet, still snoring.

Just then, Diyah's phone started to buzz. It was Danita. Diyah sent her to voicemail. "Why is she calling so much lately? I don't want to talk to her right now," she said out loud. Diyah's phone buzzed again, but this time, it was Rah, her coworker who'd she had grown fond of in these past few months. Diyah eagerly picks up the phone, "Hey, Rah, you trying to go out tonight? I feel like partying!" And just like that, Diyah had plans for the night. She had to get herself out of the rut of her past and escape it, if only for a few hours.

Chapter 2
Trigger Warning

Danita Franklin sits up, right in her king-sized bed, rubbing her stomach, which has gained a little weight recently. Danita is 32 years old, 5'7", a russet brown complected woman with freckles on her cheekbones. She had black curly kinky hair that was currently styled in double-strand twist underneath her black satin bonnet. She had full lips, and her full figure carried her 220lbs in all the right places. She smiled affectionately. Only she and her husband, Amir, knew she was pregnant. They planned to announce it to their family over dinner this upcoming Sunday, now that she was approaching 14 weeks and would be in her second trimester. Danita was hoping her sister Diyah would come, but she hadn't been able to get her to answer any of her calls lately. Danita was hurt by her sister's distance over the past 11 months because neither of them was aware of the truth about their family dynamic. Danita sighs and decides that she will not let Diyah steal her joy. She looks over lovingly at her husband, Amir, who had begun to stir from his alarm. Amir is 33 years old, 6'5", Hershey Chocolate, dark brown eyes, and weighs 250lbs. He had black, kinky, curly hair like hers, which he wore in a high taper fade, and he had a full beard.

"Good morning, baby," Danita says.

"Good morning, Sunshine," Amir says as he sits up to kiss her after turning his alarm off. "How's my wife and little lemon this morning?" Amir begins to rub Danita's stomach.

Danita laughs. She loved how Amir had been keeping up with the size of their baby as it grew weekly. "It's almost a peach at this point. We're fine."

"Good. That's music to my ears this morning. I'm surprised you're still in bed. You're going to work, right?"

"Yes, I'm about to get up now. I was just in my thoughts this morning."

"I thought you just said you were fine?"

"I am fine," Danita reassured him. "I was just thinking about Diyah. I want her here with us, too, on Sunday. She should be present for this announcement."

"I know, sweetheart. All you can do is invite her. Text her and invite her. After that, you've done all you can do."

"It's just that it's been almost a year. That's the frustrating part, but you're right. I'll text her and invite her," Danita responds as she gets up to go use the bathroom in their ensuite.

"Sweetheart, how about I make breakfast for you and the little lemon peach this morning?" Amir suggested as he began to get out of bed himself and stretch. "Baby, did you hear me?" Amir calls to Danita in the bathroom.

"Amir!" Danita yells in a shrieking tone. Amir rushes into the bathroom to see Danita looking into the toilet, crying. Amir looks inside and sees what she's staring at. Blood.

"No, no, no, no, no!" Amir says as he shakes his head. "We have to get you to the hospital! Come on, let's get you dressed." Amir guides Danita out of the bathroom after helping her clean up some of the blood. "Come on, sweetheart. We gotta go. Everything could be fine, but we need to go now," he says urgently.

Danita felt like she was about to lose control. She looks up at Amir, teary-eyed. "You think the baby's ok? You think it could be fine?" She asked earnestly.

"Yes, sweetheart, but we need to go and get y'all checked out. Do you need me to help you get dressed?"

" I-I-I can dress myself," she stutters.

Thirty minutes later, Amir and Danita arrived at their local emergency room. Danita had been triaged, and she'd provided a urinalysis. An ultrasound was completed, and she was in the examination room, lying back on the bed, awaiting the doctor's results. Amir was standing by the bedside, holding her hand.

"It says online that it could be a urinary tract infection bae," Amir showed Danita his phone.

"I don't know Amir. I want to think the best, but as I lie here and think, my breasts are no longer sore, and I haven't had morning sickness in a few days. I'm now experiencing some bad cramps," she said with tears in her eyes and a lump in her throat.

"What are you saying? Those symptoms could have subsided because you are approaching your second trimester. Cramps are common with a UTI. Speak life, baby. Just wait for the doctor. Everything will be fine, you'll see. Let's pray together." Amir prayed, placing his hand over Danita's stomach.

Thirty more minutes passed before the doctor arrived. Danita shivered when she came in. The doctor's presence created a chilling atmosphere. She rubbed her upper arms in a helpless attempt to warm herself up. The doctor was a slender African-American woman who looked to be in her 50s. "Mr. and Mrs. Franklin? I'm Dr. Johnson." She extends her hand to shake Danita's. Danita's hand was shaking. Dr. Johnson then turned to shake Amir's hand.

"Dr. Johnson, I don't mean to be rude, but what are the results? It's a UTI or something like that, right?" Amir asked, searching Dr. Johnson's eyes.

"Unfortunately, the ultrasound showed no signs of a heartbeat. I'm sorry to say it, but it looks like you are miscarrying, Mrs.Franklin. I'm extremely sorry for your loss. I can answer questions at this time or give you a few moments if you would like?"

Danita begins to sob. Amir's shoulders drooped. He consoles Danita. After a few moments, he then turns his attention back to the doctor. "Is there not anything that can be done?" Amir pleaded with a high-pitched voice as he continued to console Danita.

"Unfortunately, nothing can be done to stop this process; however, we do have options to make your wife comfortable during this time. Again, you two have my sincerest condolences. I'm sorry this is happening. I know this is hard to accept, and it won't make you feel any better to know, but this is common."

After a few minutes of silence, Dr. Johnson addressed Danita, "You mentioned to the nurses that you are experiencing some pain. We can prescribe something for your pain, Mrs. Franklin. We have some support resources too to help during this time. Your body has begun this process naturally, and you can follow up with your OBGyn. That's Wilson County OBGyn, correct? Would you like me to call you in that prescription? If so, I need to confirm any allergies and which pharmacy." Danita continued to cry and ignored Dr. Johnson.

"Yes, that's her provider. Please call her something in, to the pharmacy noted in her chart. No known allergies", Amir responded quietly for his wife.

"Ok, we will get that sent in electronically. And I'll return in a few moments with discharge instructions and a follow-up appointment at Wilson County OBGyn. I'll also include an insert for what to expect as time passes, but we'll review that before you leave. I'll be right back." Before exiting the room, Dr. Johnson rubs Danita's back and gives Amir a nod. Amir continues to hold Danita as she continues to sob on his chest. She was holding him tightly because the chill she felt earlier was now piercing through her bones. The examination room had become their crypt. Amir held Danita closely as he was choking back tears himself.

Two hours later, Amir and Danita were back home in their kitchen after being discharged from the hospital and picking up Danita's prescription. Danita was no longer crying; however, her eyes were bloodshot red. She had not said a word to Amir.

"Can I get you anything, sweetheart?" Amir asked in a hoarse voice.

"No." She paused. "How are you? I haven't checked in on you. I'm sorry."

"I'm confused. I don't understand why this happened. Is God punishing me for abandoning my child?" He was referring to the child he had from a previous relationship.

"No, God isn't punishing you. And, you didn't abandon your child. You were a teen father who decided to place your child in adoption care with a family who was ready for them. I thought He was punishing me for my deceit last year, but then I remembered that this is common, which is why I didn't want to share with our family and others until my second trimester. This just wasn't our time, unfortunately, but truthfully, I don't understand it either."

"I'm angry," Amir responded. "This isn't fair. I've lost two kids."

"I understand. You have the right to be angry," Danita consoled him. "We'll get through this together." Just then, Danita saw the six-week ultrasound posted on the fridge and began to cry again. Amir held her tightly and consoled her. "I can't breathe," Danita gasped. She was experiencing a panic attack.

"I got you, I got you. Focus on your breaths. Breathe in deeply for 3 seconds, hold for 3 seconds, and exhale slowly for 3 seconds," Amir guided Danita as he fought back his own tears. Amir held Danita until she calmed down, and then she was able to go shower. Then, Amir removed the ultrasound from the refrigerator and began collecting all the reminders of their pregnancy around the home for safekeeping. As he stored the ultrasound, "Our Baby's First Seven Years" record book, all the items included in Danita's 1st trimester pregnancy gift box, and a small teddy bear, Amir found hot tears beginning to stream down his face. For the first time since leaving their home that morning, he allowed himself to acknowledge and release his own emotions.

Chapter 3
The Discovery

Diyah was sitting on her living room couch, wearing a white oversized V-neck and black leggings. She hangs up the phone with her sister, Danita. She learned that her sister was pregnant, but now she had miscarried. Diyah felt so guilty because she had been ignoring her sister's calls. She now knew that originally, Danita wanted to invite her over for the big announcement, but the most recent calls were to share the loss. Diyah recalled the pain and sadness in Danita's voice. Diyah apologized for distancing herself and committed to being a better sister. Diyah understood that her sister and brother-in-law needed all their family at this time; however, Diyah was unsure if she could honor her sister's request and join them for Thanksgiving this year.

Diyah looked over at her end table. The letter her mother had sent the previous year was lying there, unopened, waiting for her. Diyah took a deep breath and decided that if she was going to consider Thanksgiving with the family, she needed to open the letter. Diyah reached for the envelope. She noticed her hands started to shake, and she felt nauseous, but she opened the envelope anyway and began to read. Diyah was surprised to see that the letter was short. Her mom apologized again in the letter and asked for Diyah's forgiveness. Her mother reiterated that she was experiencing postpartum depression and felt isolated after giving birth to Danita. Daisy wrote that she needed an outlet and adult connection, which is what led her to having a moment of weakness resulting in Diyah's conception. Daisy reiterated how much Diyah was loved by she and Dawson, and that her name meant "love" in Lembaama, although it is spelt differently. Daisy expressed that Dawson feared Diyah would one day learn the truth and reject him, which is why he kept a certain distance from her despite how much he loved her. Diyah began to cry because she had done exactly what Dawson feared. Diyah also learned from the letter that her biological father's name was and that he had relocated to Knightdale as a business owner, the last time Daisy heard.

Diyah typed in her biological father's name into a Google search engine. She gasped when she saw a picture of her biological father. Diyah continued to cry. She questioned how a man could deny his child, let alone a child who looked so much like him. Diyah clicked on the hyperlink to what appeared to be her biological father's business page. She confirmed it was his business page. She read his bio and saw more pictures.

"He has a family!" Diyah screamed and threw her phone at the wall. Both of her cats ran away from her as the thud startled them. She knew she'd most likely cracked her screen, but she did not care. She sat still for a few moments, feeling her heart pound in her chest. Then, a devious smile spread across Diyah's face. She realized she needed a stress reliever. She wiped tears from her face, grabbed her keys and brown sweater, slid on her old black UGGs, and picked up her phone off the floor. Surprisingly, her case protected her screen and there were no damages. She entered an address into her GPS to guide her to a nearby gym.

Twenty minutes later, Diyah was sitting outside her destination. She looked at the building. It was a gray building with glass doors and windows covering the entire front. She noticed that it was easy to identify with the name written in bright red letters. "Sánchez Rivera Gym", she read to herself out loud. She sat in her Chevy pickup truck contemplating whether she was really about to go in. The idea seemed so clear when she was at home, but now that she was here, she wasn't so sure. Diyah observed her surroundings. She observed diversity in terms of race and age among the clientele entering and exiting the gym.

"Just go on in and get a tour," she encouraged herself out loud. Diyah slowly gets out of her truck; her legs feel like Jello. She walked through the entrance and made her way to the customer service desk. Afrobeats was playing throughout the speakers in the gym.

"Welcome to Sánchez Rivera Gym. How may we help you?" The young attendant greeted Diyah.

He was a Caucasian male who looked to be in his late teens, with brown eyes and brown hair styled in a crew cut low fade. He was wearing a red Sánchez Rivera polo with black joggers. She read his name badge. "Hi, Jamie. My name is Diyah Jones, and I'm interested in joining the gym. Can someone give me a tour and tell me what makes your gym unique?"

"Sí. Just give me a few minutes, and I'd be glad to take you on that tour," Jamie responded.

Diyah looked around inside the gym. She observed that the setup was typical of most gyms: weights, a cardio section, stationary cycles, stomach machines, arm machines, and leg machines. She saw that classes were offered too. She noticed that mostly everything was written in English and Spanish, and she noticed that levántate! in red letters was displayed on each wall.

"Ready?" Jamie asked, interrupting her self-observation.

"Yes, please take the lead."

"So what are the goals you'd like to target with gym membership?"

"I want to maintain my physical health. I'm getting older, I'll be 30 next year, and I need to make exercise a part of my routine to manage my weight as my metabolism slows. I'm 165lbs and I'd like to maintain this weight. Also, I've had some recent personal stress, so working out would give me a healthy outlet."

"I understand. Let's start over here in our classrooms. Cardio is a great way to address your target health goals. We offer Zumba classes. We offer boxing & Pilates classes too, both are great ways to relieve stress. Do any of these classes sound of interest to you?"

"Yes. I think Zumba would be a fun way to get in some cardio, and boxing would help me release some stress."

"Great! I'd recommend any of our classes. We have some great instructors. You asked initially what made our gym unique. Most gyms don't have the diversity in culture that our gym has. Ninety-seven percent of our staff are bilingual, speaking both English and Spanish. We offer three classes several times a week at different times to accommodate different schedules. Also, several members of our staff are cross-trained, so classes or personal training sessions are rarely rescheduled due to staffing."

"I see. Sounds appealing," Diyah smiled.

"Oh, here's one of our personal trainers now. And, he's one of our boxing instructors, too."

Diyah observed a Mexican-American man walking in their direction. He was distracted on the phone. She was surprised as he got closer that he was younger than she'd expected. He looked to be in his mid-50s, he was about 5'5", with hazel eyes, and brown colored wavy hair styled in a wolf cut. He was wearing the Sánchez Rivera white polo with black joggers.

"Miguel!" Jamie waved him over.

The man ended his phone call and headed directly for Diyah and Jamie. He extended his hand to Diyah. "Hola. I'm Miguel. Welcome to Sánchez Rivera Gym," he greeted her.

"Hey, I'm Diyah Jones. I came in today to tour the gym," Diyah beamed.

"I'm just giving her the tour and educating her on the gym," Jamie offered to Miguel.

"Well, you're in good hands with Jamie. He's been with us since he was a Sophomore in high school, which makes him a knowledgeable employee. Any questions that I might answer for you personally, Ms. Jones?" Miguel asked.

"I'm sure I'll have plenty of questions in the future, but not today. It was a pleasure meeting you," Diyah continued to smile.

"Very well. I hope to see you around soon," Miguel smiled, shaking Diyah's hand again. "If you would excuse me."

"How often is he here? Diyah asked Jamie as Miguel walked off. "You mentioned not having any staffing issues. I want to make sure I can get my boxing classes in."

"Miguel is here most days, but we have other boxing instructors too," Jamie responded. "Do you have any other questions? If not, we can continue our tour."

"Actually, no, and I've decided. I'd like to get a membership today," Diyah stated while flashing Jamie her million-dollar smile.

"Wonderful!" Jamie grinned widely with pride. "Follow me this way, and we'll get you registered, and once you've downloaded our app, you can see all our classes and their days and times. Fifteen minutes later, Diyah was a member of Sánchez Rivera Gym. She exited the gym with butterflies in her stomach and a grin on her face.

Chapter 4
Daddy's Lil' Girl

Thursday, November 16th. Diyah yawns. She's just waking up for the day. She looks at the date and time on her phone. It was eleven in the morning. She realized she had turned her alarm off and went back to sleep for an extra hour. She scolded herself for oversleeping again. With Christmas approaching next month, she had decided she needed to increase her door dashing to make some Holiday cash. Her plan was to door dash during lunchtime today. She'd gotten about 4 hours of sleep after closing the bar earlier that morning, and she felt exhausted. She always felt tired. She sat up and began to reflect on her plan for the day. She knew she needed to call and check in on Danita and Amir, as it had been a couple of days, but she didn't want to be asked about Thanksgiving, given it was a week away. Diyah was thankful that Danita had not mentioned it again, but she was nervous that she would. Diyah wanted to be there for her sister and brother-in-law, but she was not ready to see her mother and Dawson. Danita did let on that Dawson would be joining them for Thanksgiving. *A lot has changed since last year,* she thought to herself.

Diyah looked at her phone again. 11:07 AM. She needed to wash her face, brush her teeth, and put on her almond-brown T-shirt and black workout leggings as she planned to go to Zumba at the gym after door dashing through the lunch rush. This would be her third time going to the gym since she'd joined. Diyah continued to reflect as she prepared for her day. She thought about the information she'd learned about her biological father, how he was living life as if she did not exist. She wondered if he ever thought about her. Diyah felt her heart rate speeding up; she could hear the pulses beating in her ears. Her face became warm. She allowed her mind to shift to her plan. Then, she thought about Dawson. She pitied him, and she hated that she did; she wanted to stay angry at him, too. Diyah realized that she might be ready to forgive Dawson for keeping the truth from her, but she was confused about her lack of desire to see him and her mother for Thanksgiving. *Am I ready to forgive if I'm avoiding*? She thought to herself. She stood in her hallway leading to her front door and looked at herself in the mirror she had mounted on the wall. She looked tired, and her hair, which was currently pulled back in a frizzy ponytail, was in desperate need of a shampoo and deep conditioner. She threw on an almond brown plain baseball cap covering her hair. In that moment, she decided that she needed to vent. Her coworker, Rah, was always there when she wanted to party, but it was time to see if she was good at listening and being supportive. Diyah headed out the door to her first pick up at Zaxby's. She decided to call Danita on her way to the first delivery drop-off, giving her a reason to rush off the phone, and she would talk to Rah later that night at work.

Two and a half hours later, Diyah was walking through the doors to Sánchez Rivera Gym. She was feeling less stressed from earlier. She called Danita and Amir, and thankfully, neither answered her call. She felt guilty for being thankful that they didn't answer, but she couldn't deny that she was thankful. She stretched while looking around the gym. She felt disappointed. She slowly walked into the Zumba area. Their instructor, Sophia, began yelling levántate! which Diyah had come to learn to mean "get up!" And just like that, they began their warmup to *La Terraza* by Gustavo Elis. Forty-five minutes later, Diyah was walking out of her Zumba class when she bumped into Miguel. He was wearing a white polo with the gym's logo and black joggers.

"Perdon," Miguel apologized.

"No, excuse me. I wasn't paying attention," Diyah responded.

"No worries, Diyah. You're just coming out of Zumba, I see. Did you enjoy the class?"

"You remembered my name?" Diyah questioned and smiled.

"Sí. I make it my business to learn the regulars, and I see that you have visited the gym a few times since joining.

"Oh, yes. Well, I am enjoying Zumba."

"Muy Bien. I'll see you around soon. Take care."

"Bye," Diyah said to Miguel as he was making his way to his office.

Diyah climbed into her Chevy pickup moments later and turned on the radio to the local station. *Authorities have now learned from an eyewitness report that the FC Attacker is approximately 5'9" to 5'10" tall, with a slim build, and wears all-black clothing, including a black hoodie, black ski mask, black pants, and black leather gloves. Authorities are asking that if you see anyone matching this description, please take caution and call 911.* Diyah turned her radio off and looked out of her window. She saw Miguel coming outside to greet a teenage Latina who looked to be 19 or 20 years old. She was light-skinned, with long, wavy brown hair that had caramel honey blonde highlights that was parted down the middle. She was wearing an oversized, dark green button-up cardigan sweater, a black turtleneck tucked into wide-leg, multi-colored patchwork jeans, and black western block-heeled cowgirl boots. Diyah noted that she was not carrying a gym bag, suggesting she was not coming to work out. She observed how happy the two looked as Miguel kissed her on the cheek and let her walk through the gym entrance first. *That must be his daughter*, Diyah thought to herself. The inside of Diyah ached. She yearned for that attention from her father. All of her life, Dawson was emotionally distant from her, and her biological father did not want anything to do with her. *Maybe if I talked to him, he'd embrace me like he does Danita. Is that stupid? Ma did say that he kept his distance all these years out of fear,* Diyah thought to herself. Just then, her phone started to buzz, distracting her from her thoughts.

Hey sis, how are you and Amir?" Diyah asked, answering the phone. It was Danita finally returning her call from earlier. Diyah was pleased to be pulled from her thoughts.

"Hey. There are ok moments and there are bad moments. We're taking it one day at a time. That's all we can do. I've been making sure to get in some sunlight daily to aid with my mood. Thanks for checking. How are you?"

"I'm ok, I guess. I'm trying to figure some things out. Mentally, I'm all over the place. I've been stuck, you know."

"Yeah, I do. Listen, Diyah, you know I would love to have you over for Thanksgiving, but if you're not ready, a part of me understands.

As much as we would like to put a time frame on our feelings, that's easier said than done. I have more clarity about that now."

"I appreciate you for understanding. How about I come over before or after Thanksgiving? I can cook whatever you two would like. How does that sound?"

"That sounds like a great idea. I'll check with Amir about a date and get back with you."

"Anything else I can do?" Diyah asked.

"Just keep being present and take care of you. It's good to hear from you, Diyah, despite the circumstances.I've missed you."

"I've missed you, too. I'll see you soon. I love you."

"I love you more. Later."

"Later." Diyah hung up the phone, added a few items to her Amazon cart, and checked out before heading home to shower and rest before her night shift began.

———————

"Hey, Rah, you here yet?" Diyah asked, answering her phone. It was Sunday afternoon, and Diyah invited Rah over to talk because they hadn't had a chance to on Thursday night during their shift.

"I'm in the apartment complex, but I can't find your building."

Looking out the window, "Oh, I see you. Come straight on down and look to your left. I'm the building with the graffiti and moss growing up the side."

"Ok, I see you looking out the window. Go on and open up the door, it's cold outchea."

A few minutes later, Diyah heard footsteps getting closer. She looks out of her peephole and opens the door before Rah can knock. "Welcome to my home," Diyah greeted Rah while taking her burnt orange hoodie that Rah had just pulled off to hang. "Thanks for coming. Have a seat." Diyah motioned her hand towards her couch. "Would you like anything to drink? I can make some cocoa or tea if you need to warm up."

"I'm good, thanks. Now what do you want to talk about? And where are those cats? I don't want them sneaking up on me?" Rah began to look around, feeling a little anxious. She finally sat down on Diyah's dark teal faux leather couch, opposite Diyah. Rah was 5'9", with a tawny brown skin complexion, dark brown eyes and long dark hair that she had pulled back into a bun. She was wearing a black Cincinnati Bengals game jersey tucked into her gray high-rise stretch skinny jeans and Safety Orange Nike Air Max 90 sneakers. "It doesn't smell like you have cats," Rah commented.

"I keep the litter boxes clean, chile, and they're in my bedroom, don't worry, they're not going to bother you," Diyah reassured Rah. "Girl, I just need to vent. My life has changed so much since last year. You know I haven't been at the bar that much longer than you."

"How has your life changed? What were you doing before?" Rah asked.

"I was a traveling RN."

"No wonder you're bougee," Rah laughed. "How did you end up working at the bar? And living here?" Rah looked around Diyah's apartment, emphasizing her question.

"It's a long story," Diyah responded. Diyah then shared with Rah the events that took place from Thanksgiving last year to the present. She also shared who her biological father was with Rah, but omitted her plan that she was contemplating.

"Girl! That's a lot. So what are you going to do? Are you going to confront your biological father?"

"I plan to, yeah. I keep waiting until I have the nerve, but I think I'm going to just do it. He's the one I truly need to talk to, not my mother or Dawson."

"Yeah, I feel you. You should talk to him. But listen, have you considered how Dawson didn't have to do anything for you? He signed your birth certificate, knowing you weren't his child. He took care of you. How many guys will do that? I understand you are hurt by the secret he and your mom kept, but if you ask me, the good they've done far outweighs that one secret. Let it go with them. It's been a year already, but your biological father, that's a different story altogether."

"I blame my mother more than Dawson. I feel like I can let it go with him sooner rather than later, but my mom, that still stings."

"I hear you. Your mom's shame motivated her decision not to reveal her secret. Ain't you ever done anything that you're ashamed of, bougee? Lord knows I have." Rah gives Diyah a side eye.

Diyah laughed. "Yes, I have. I guess I never thought about it like that. A mother is supposed to be a role model; it's not easy admitting that kind of mistake to their child."

"No, it's not easy, but they love you. Your mom kept you despite the possibility you weren't her husband's, and your daddy took care of you. Dawson is your daddy, you know? That's a good man if you ask me."

"Yes, I know. And, you're right about all of this. Wow, Rah, I didn't know you had this side to you."

"It's obvious we don't know each other that well, but don't forget I am 33, which makes me wiser than your 29 years of life. Besides, life has taught me a few things. Hey, do you mind if I use your bathroom?"

"Sure. It's down the hall, first door on your left." As Rah got up to go use the restroom, she accidentally tripped over one of Diyah's open Amazon packages in the hallway. "You good girl? My bad, I opened that box and left it right there."

"Yeah, but Diyah, what's this?" Rah asked, looking confused. She was holding a black hoodie, a ski mask, black leather gloves, and black jogging pants. "Why do you have this? Isn't this what the FC Attacker has been described to be wearing by eyewitness reports?"

Chapter 5
Draw the Veil

Diyah laughs nervously. "Yeah, I ordered that. I'm preparing for Halloween next year. You know that costume will be perfect for next year."

Rah stares at Diyah. "Diyah, what's going on? Obviously, you're more upset about all of this than I thought. Are you the FC Attacker?" Rah whispers.

"God no!" Diyah responded. She got up from her couch and began to pace away from Rah. Turning to face Rah again, she admitted, "I have considered attacking my biological father, though."

"So let me get this straight. You're saying that you're not the FC Attacker, but you were going to assault your biological father and hope the FC Attacker is blamed?" Rah balled her fist tight by her sides.

"I hadn't thought about it like that. Why are you getting upset? I didn't know you cared so much for strangers," Diyah laughs nervously, trying to make light of the situation. "Look, I'm just so angry, Rah. I haven't been completely honest." Diyah sits back down, motions for Rah to sit too, and then shares the rest of her truth with Rah.

When Diyah finished, Rah shook her head at her. She did not speak immediately. After a few moments, she responded, "Honey, you're almost just as messed up as me. Your sperm donor is a deadbeat. I'm not judging you, but listen, get rid of these clothes you have, hear? Right now, you're good, but if you go down this path, there's no going back. Trust me, I know. Stay away from this if you can't control yourself."

"Yeah, maybe I should write him a letter if I can't confront him without aggression."

"Sounds like a plan. Listen, I have to go, my team is playing at 4 PM. Talk to your mom and *your dad*. I'm sure that'll help you with this anger." Rah begins to gather her things and walks towards the door.

"I will soon. Thanks, Rah, for listening and not judging me. I hope this will stay between us, especially, well, you know."

"I got you, don't worry. We all have secrets we don't want to get out, myself included. But seriously, heed my warning."

"I will. Thanks again. We'll talk soon."

"Diyah, if you do decide to go through with your plan. I don't know anything, do you understand?"

"Yes, I understand. I won't go through with it, though. I promise."

"Ok, girl, bye," Rah said, hugging Diyah.

"Bye."

After Rah left, Diyah checked the time. The gym closed at 5 pm on Sundays; therefore, she had time to get in a run on the treadmill to clear her head. She quickly changed into her gray workout leggings and gray "I'm Not Short" hoodie to head out the door. An hour later, she had finished a quick run on the treadmill. She was wearing her AirPods, tuning out the Afrobeats playing at the gym. DMX, LL Cool J, and Crime Mob had her adrenaline pumped. She decided she would lift some weights. She was currently listening to *The Monster* by Eminem ft Rihanna. After she finished a set, she saw Miguel walking into his office. She looked around. She and one other person were the only two there as it was near closing. T.I. *U Don't Know Me* began playing next on her playlist. She smiled, cut her music off, gathered her things, and walked towards Miguel's office.

"Hey Miguel," she said as she stood at his office door. "Mind if I come in?" Miguel was wearing his standard Sánchez Rivera white polo shirt, paired with black joggers and all-black Adidas running shoes. Diyah began to look around at Miguel's certificates, other accolades, and family pictures he had posted.

"Hola Diyah, sí, come on in. What can I do for you?"

"I was wondering if you ever think about your firstborn child?"

"Marisol?" Miguel asked with a bright smile. "Yes, I think about her all the time. She is a freshman in college and the light of my life. Have you seen her around here?"

"No, not Marisol. Your *first*born. You had a child before her, correct?"

Miguel began to shake his head in confusion. "Excuse me? Listen, Diyah, I'm not quite sure what kind of game you're playing. It's now 5, and I need to close the gym. I'm going to have to ask you to leave now."

"I'm not playing any game. I'm your daughter, Miguel. Look at me! Marisol and I favor don't you agree?" Diyah was breathing heavy. She picks up a picture of Marisol from Miguel's desk and holds it next to her face.

"I don't have any other children. Is this a scam or something? Listen, I suggest you get your things and leave. Please don't return to this gym."

"I'm not leaving until I get some answers!" Diyah yelled. "I want to know why you didn't want to be in my life. Think back almost 30 years ago. Don't you remember a lady by the name of Daisy Jones? You were just a personal trainer back then. You trained her." Just then, Diyah saw guilt come across Miguel's face.

"I'm going to call the police if you don't leave," Miguel responded, voice quavering.

"I know you recognized the name. You told her that you would step up and take responsibility if you were my father, some lie that turned out to be. Now I want to know why? Why didn't you step up?" Diyah moved in closer to Miguel's desk.

"This is the last time I'm going to ask you, Diyah. Please leave."

"You're not even going to admit that I'm your child?" Diyah asked, tears had filled her eyes. "It seems like you've forgotten all about me. I don't want anything from you but answers. Don't you want to know about me?"

"I want you to leave," Miguel responded coldly, looking at Diyah straight into her eyes. His finger was pointing towards the exit.

Tears began to fall down Diyah's face. In a rage, she knocked everything off Miguel's desk. He attempted to walk around the desk to exit, but she pushed the desk forward to corner him in. She knocked certificates off the wall and broke all of his family pictures. She threw a stack chair at his head. He ducked out of the way. She screamed. She stared at Miguel as he stood looking back at her with his hands up. She noticed that he had turned a shade lighter. His complexion was almost as white as his polo shirt. He was shaking just like she was, but she felt in control. She thought about her plan. "You're going to pay for this," Diyah promised calmly, pointing at Miguel. She gathered her things, ran out of his office and the gym, slamming the door behind her. She noticed that the other person had left. She hoped they'd left before the commotion began.

The next morning, Diyah awoke feeling horrible. She looks at her phone. It was 7:45 AM. She is never up this early nowadays unless she can't sleep. She reflected on her actions from the previous night; it felt like a nightmare. *It was like an out-of-body experience,* she thought to herself. She could not believe she acted in such a rage. Once she got home last night and calmed down, she felt embarrassed. She wanted answers, but she also wanted acceptance. She decided last night that she would apologize to Miguel and cover the cost of damages, but that decision made it difficult for her to sleep. She was anxious at the thought of facing him again. She had many emotions. She began to get dressed so she could head straight to the gym.

Ten minutes later, Diyah was out the door and headed to the gym. She looked disheveled, with dark circles under her eyes. She was wearing the same outfit from the evening before. Her heart began to beat fast as she drove. She practiced what she planned to say out loud, " Hi Miguel. I didn't come to start any more trouble. I'm here to apologize if you can hear me out. No." She shakes her head as she continues to drive. "Good morning, Mr. Miguel. I know I'm the last person you want to see, but I've had some time to think. Can we talk? I promise I come in peace. No, that's still not good enough." She says to herself. She tightens her grip around the steering wheel. She had her hands positioned on the steering wheel at 10 and 2 because she needed to ground herself.

Fifteen minutes later, she pulled into the parking lot of Sánchez Rivera Gym. She looks at herself in the rearview mirror. She prays, "God, I need you. I'm hurt and I'm still angry, but you know that. I know I did wrong. Give me the words to say to Miguel. In Jesus' name. Amen." Diyah takes a deep breath, gets out of her truck, and slowly makes her way towards the entrance of the gym. She arrived at the glass door, but when she pulled on it, it did not budge. She noticed the gym did not appear to be open. She looked closer inside and saw Jamie. She knocked to get his attention and waved him over.

"Hey Diyah," Jamie said, opening the door. "The gym is closed today due to unforeseen circumstances. I'm in the process of printing up signs to put on the doors."

"Oh no, why is the gym closed? I was hoping to speak with Miguel."

"I don't have the details, but I know he's currently hospitalized."

"Oh my God! What happened?"

"Again, I don't have the details. I'm puzzled by it all. His office is destroyed. The police came by asking questions. I just did what Mrs. Rivera asked and closed the gym today. I don't know when we'll be open, Diyah. This is all just messed up." Jamie said with his voice cracking. "I've been working for Miguel for years, you know? Nothing like this has ever happened. This is a nice neighborhood."

"Why did the police come by? Was his hospitalization caused by illegal activity?"

"I guess so. Listen, Diyah, I have to get back. I'm sorry you drove out this way. You'll get a notification when we reopen, okay? We just hadn't gotten a chance to send out a memo through the app."

"Okay. Thanks, Jamie. I'm sorry about all of this."

"Bye, Diyah."

"Bye, take care." Diyah began walking back towards her pickup truck. Thoughts and questions were circling her mind. She hated to admit it, but she was happy Miguel was hospitalized. He'd hurt her by not being in her life, and then denying her last night was the ultimate hurt. "God doesn't like ugly," she said out loud as she reached her truck's door. As she climbed inside her truck, she had a change of heart. She hoped his injuries weren't life-threatening because she wanted there to be another opportunity for them. *How did this happen? What happened to him? Why are the police involved? Did someone hurt him?* Diyah thought to herself as she pulled out of the parking lot and began to drive towards home.

Chapter 6
Sisterly Love

"Hey, Diyah. It's good to see you," Danita greeted and hugged her sister standing in her entryway. Diyah had showered and changed after going to the gym earlier, only to find out about Miguel. Now she was wearing a burgundy sweater underneath a black coat, olive green tights, and her black UGGs. "Here, let me take your coat." Per their agreement, Diyah came over before Thanksgiving to avoid their parents and to provide food for Danita and Amir until Thanksgiving Day.

"Hey sis. It's good to see you, too." Diyah responded by hugging Danita back. She noticed that it looked like Danita had lost some weight, most likely from the grief. "I can hang my own coat. Go on and sit down. Can Amir bring in the food from the truck?"

"Amir!" Danita called, heading into the living room. She was wearing a leopard print moo moo and black bedroom shoes. "Diyah's here! Can you bring in the food from her truck for her, please?"

"Yes, dear! Be right there!" Amir called out from the bedroom. Danita sat down in their dark and light gray sectional. She nestled herself in the corner of the sectional's chaise and began to cover herself with a throw blanket.

"Thanks, bae!" Danita responded to Amir as she was getting comfortable. Diyah joined her sister in the family room and began to look around. She was proud of them and their success. Her brother-in-law was a top-selling real estate agent, and her sister was a 5th-grade English teacher who had been voted her school's Elementary Teacher of the Year earlier in the year. Being in Danita's home reminded Diyah of how far she'd regressed in her own life.

"Y'all painted in here?" Diyah asked as she sat down on the

sectional right next to her sister.

"Yeah, we painted around the beginning of the year," Danita responded. "We wanted a change after we reconciled."

"It looks nice. What color is that? It looks like a soft peach or pink, maybe."

"It's called Modern Love. It's peachy. We wanted the room to feel cozy."

"Well, it does. It also brings out the red undertone in your oak hardwood floor," Diyah smiled. "Share that throw blanket with me." Diyah scooted close to Danita as she was extending the throw blanket. "So how are you, and Amir?"

"We have our days. We're taking it one day at a time. We won't return to work until the beginning of the year. With all the Holiday time between Thanksgiving, Christmas, and New Year, it just makes sense. Amir decided to be home too."

"Oh, that makes sense. I'm glad you two don't have to rush back to work. How've you been coping though?"

"Different ways. I ordered this journal, *A Journey to Healing: A Guided Journal Through Loss, Grief, and Healing For Women* by Toshina S. Wiggins. I've been working through it. That's helped, along with sunlight, prayer, leaning on Amir and y'all. I looked forward to seeing you today. This brings me joy," Danita smiled.

"I'm glad to bring some joy. I'm glad to be here to support you two."

"We're happy you're here, sister-in-law. Give me a hug," Amir says, walking into the living room. He was wearing a black V-neck T-shirt, black sweatpants, and black ankle socks. Diyah stands, and she and Amir embrace. "Thanks for the food too, it smells good. You've brought more than enough."

"It was my pleasure. Y'all can freeze it if you don't eat it all before Thanksgiving," Diyah responded, sitting back down next to Danita.

"What did you bring?" Danita asks.

"Broccoli and cheddar soup and chicken and dumplings with hush puppies," Diyah beamed.

"Oh, that sounds delicious," Amir responded.

"Yes, it does, but I know you didn't cook Diyah," Danita teased.

"Actually, I did. I've had to get into cooking to save money. A lot has changed," Diyah responded.

"Tell me all about it. It'll be nice to listen to someone else for a change," Danita requested.

"That's my cue," Amir interjected. "I'll leave you girls to catch up. Danita, do you need anything before I go up to the man cave? The food is on the island in the kitchen."

"No, I'm good. Thanks, baby," Danita states. She turns to Diyah. "So, go on. Spill. What's life been like for you?"

Diyah opens up to Danita about leaving her job as a traveling RN, and having to move, which Danita already knew. She shares how she is currently financially supporting herself. Diyah specifically omits how she had opened their mother's letter and learned the identity of her biological father.

"Oh, Diyah. I hate how your life has changed in this way. Do you want it to get back on track? Danita asked.

"Yeah. I do. My current life is depressing, you know," Diyah admitted. "Like I told you, I'm stuck. I keep replaying Thanksgiving last year in my head.

"I know depression all too well," Danita assured Diyah while tearing up. "I keep having flashbacks to the blood in the toilet. When I was changing my pads every hour, the flashbacks were worse then. My emotions shift from feeling numb, angry, guilty, and anxious. I keep thinking if I did something to cause this miscarriage? I try to fight that thought, but it keeps coming back. Amir is supportive, but he's closed off when it comes to his own emotions. He doesn't want to talk about the miscarriage. I feel lonely at times because this happened to us, but it seems like I'm the only one impacted by it." Danita shook her head from side to side. "At least the bleeding and physical pain are gone. Why didn't God answer our prayers? We have faith in Him," Danita questioned as the tears continued to flow.

"Sis," Diyah handed Danita some Kleenex and consoled her. "You didn't do anything to cause this. This just unfortunately happens at times. I'm sorry. And, I can't explain why God didn't answer your prayers. This is a lot to process. Have you considered counseling?"

"I'm sorry for you too," Danita said between sobs. She wanted to shift into big sister mode. "But have you considered counseling yourself?"

"Huh?" Diyah asks, pulling away from Danita.

"You said you're stuck. I think counseling might be a good idea for both of us, sis," Danita pleaded, wiping the tears from her face. "I heard Tye Tribbett say that forgiveness is the initial decision on your emotional healing journey."

"I've actually not thought about counseling. I don't have insurance, so I can't afford it anyway," Diyah stated, looking down at the floor. "And, I don't know if I'm ready to forgive."

"They have places where sliding fee is an option," Danita suggested. She was in full-blown big sister mode now, and her tears had ceased. She welcomed Diyah's life as a distraction. "You can process your feelings of anger and hurt. But in the meantime, do what you can, like I am. Take care of you. Have you turned to God for help?"

"Recently, I've prayed. That was probably the first time that I've prayed in months."

"That's a good start. What made you pray?"

"I'd rather not say."

"Ok. Well, I hope you keep praying. As I shared before, prayer is helping me with this pregnancy loss, but there's nothing wrong with Jesus and a therapist. I'm going to look into that, and I hope you do too. In the meantime, can I share some scriptures with you?"

"Yeah, I guess it wouldn't hurt."

"Do you remember the story of Cain and Abel?"

"Of course, I do. Remember, we *both* grew up in the church? Diyah laughed. "Sunday school, church service, Bible Study, and revival were our life thanks to ma."

"Yeah, getting closer to God was how ma coped with what she'd done and her divorce. That's why our life was church," Danita explained.

"Oh, I didn't know that."

"Anyways, God warned Cain. He saw his heart. In **Genesis 4:7 NIV**, God told Cain that he must rule over his anger. As you recall, Cain didn't, and he ended up killing his own brother. You don't want your anger to lead you into doing something you deeply regret, so you must rule over it."

Diyah looked away from Danita because she had already allowed her anger to lead her into doing something she deeply regretted. "No, I don't want that."

"And, **Colossians 3:8 KJV** reminds us that anger doesn't come alone. It comes with *wrath, malice, blasphemy, and filthy communication.* I know you don't want anger's siblings to develop, do you, Diyah?"

"No, I don't want any of it," Diyah says softly.

"Diyah, I'm just giving you the word. I'm not trying to overwhelm you. I just want to encourage you to deal with your anger. **Ephesians 4:26-27 KJV** says, *be ye angry, and sin not: let not the sun go down upon your wrath: neither give place to the devil.* Look at this FC Attacker person from the news. Have you heard about him?"

43

"Yes, I have," Diyah gulped. "And, I know you mean well. I do want to deal with my anger, but that means I have to forgive, and like I said, I'm not ready for that. I'm really angry," She said matter-of-factly.

"You mean you're really hurt. Diyah, I was hurt by our parents, too, which made me angry, but then I remembered my own dirty little secret. My own sin. We all stand in need of forgiveness, sis. I forgave because I want to be forgiven by our Lord."

"Yes, that's true. I just need more time, Danita."

"Ok, I won't push anymore today. Life is precious and it's short, I just want my family back together, that's all. Do you mind if I email you some more scriptures in a day or two?"

"Yes, that's fine. How do you know these specific scriptures so well anyways? You're giving the book, chapter, and verse like you're a pastor," Diyah laughed, trying to lighten the mood.

"Remember, anger is a part of grief. I've gotten angry with God and myself since this miscarriage. I've even gotten angry with Amir's emotional distance. I am ruling over my own anger, but I'm a work in progress."

"I understand. Hey, do you want a little something to eat?" Diyah asked, changing the subject. "I can fix it. I can check to see if Amir wants something too. Then we can watch a movie."

"That sounds nice, Diyah. I'd like some chicken and dumplings with hush puppies, just a little bit though. Thank you for being here, supporting us, and hearing me out, too. I love you."

"I love you, too, big sis. Let me go check in on Amir," Diyah says, getting up and heading for Amir's man cave. Diyah walked slowly as she was thinking about how wrath had caused her to act out of character. *How far have I gone?* She thought to herself.

Chapter 7
Bosom of Fools

Knock. Knock. Knock. "Now, who could that be?" Diyah said out loud. She was just getting ready to climb into bed to nap before her shift at the bar later that night. Diyah knew it would be packed at the bar because it was the night before Thanksgiving. She throws on her light gray cat cartoon graphic flannel fleece robe and quietly walks to the door. She assumes it's a neighbor or someone at the wrong apartment, and she plans to pretend not to be home if either is the case.

Knock. Knock. Knock. "Ms. Jones, it's Knightdale Police Department," she heard a voice calling out from the outside of her door. Diyah froze. Her heart started pounding. *Girl, just open the door. You have nothing to be afraid of except being a black woman in her home,* she thought to herself sarcastically. Diyah proceeds to her front door, glances at herself in the hallway mirror, and then unlocks her door. She greets the officer standing before her. The officer was a Caucasian male, stood 6'1", had blue eyes, and appeared to be in his late 30s. He had blonde hair in a military cut and a slim physique. He wore a navy blue blazer, a white button-up shirt, khaki brown pants, and brown Resment Korver Sketchers. He looked as if all of his clothes were dry-cleaned and pressed professionally.

"Yes, officer. Who are you looking for? Diyah questions.

"It's actually Detective Peter Mills, ma'am," he extends his hand to shake Diyah's while showing his badge with his left hand. "Are you Ms. Diyah Jones? May I come in?"

"Yes, I'm Diyah Jones." She shakes the Detective's hand firmly. "May I ask what this is about? I was actually getting ready to lie down before work," she says as she pulls her robe closer together.

"I have some questions involving an assault that took place three nights ago. This conversation would be a lot warmer if I could come in," he suggests with a charming smile.

"I'm just fine talking right here, thank you. I don't know anything about an assault. When did you say this happened?"

"Three nights ago, ma'am. Do you know Miguel Sánchez Rivera?"

Play it cool, Diyah, she thought to herself. "The owner of Sánchez Rivera Gym? Yes, I do."

"Are you aware that he was assaulted on Sunday night?"

"Oh my God! No! I went to the gym on Monday morning and learned it was closed and he was hospitalized, but I wasn't informed why. How is he? Is he okay?"

"We have a witness statement and camera footage that you were the last person at the gym on Sunday night. In fact, we were told that you went into Mr. Rivera's office right before closing. What did y'all discuss?"

"That's personal."

"Ms. Jones. Let me be straight with you. Mr. Rivera was in a coma; however, he has recently awakened. Once the doctor clears him for some questioning, we will be speaking with Mr. Rivera. I'm here to get your side of the story. Camera footage caught you running from his office in a hurry. What was that all about?"

"Detective Mills. I had nothing to do with Mr. Rivera's assault, and I have nothing else to say. I hope he feels better soon. At this time, I'm going to shut my door. You have a nice evening."

"That's how you want to play this, Ms. Jones?" He pressed.

"Yes. I have nothing else to say," Diyah responded firmly.

"Ok. I'm sure I'll be seeing you around. Here's my card in case you change your mind. Remember, it's only a matter of time before I speak with Mr. Rivera."

"Thank you," Diyah says as she takes Detective Mills' card and closes her door. She stands behind the door and leans against it for support. She begins to breathe slowly through her nose and out through her mouth. She listens to hear his footsteps walking away. "They have nothing on you, girl. Chill," she says to herself. *Obviously, there is no camera inside his office. Surely Miguel will straighten this out. He's my father after all. That's what fathers do, right? God, I hope he'll be ok.* Diyah continued to ponder.

She slowly walks back to her bedroom. Jaylen and Sierra are staring at her. They were waiting for her to climb into bed. She looks out of her bedroom window and sees Detective Mills reach his car. He was driving a black Dodge Charger. She watches him leave. Her breaths had evened out. She walks over to her bed, removes her robe, places it at the end of the bed, and climbs in between Jaylen and Sierra because neither will move out of her way. "I'm too keyed up to sleep, kitties," she says to the cats. Sierra looks at her and yawns. She picks up her phone, she notices her hand is shaking, and she sees she has an email from Danita. She opens the email and begins to read.

Hey Sis,

I hope you're well. Here's the email I promised. We know that anger is a natural emotion, but when it causes us to sin, then it becomes a problem, right? I'm ruling over my anger because I don't want it to cause me to sin. I don't want your anger to cause you to sin either, baby sis. Anger can cause anybody to yell, say mean things, curse, become aggressive, fight, kill, refuse to forgive, separate and/or cause division. God doesn't want us to engage in these acts. Here are the scriptures:

Galatians 5:17-21 NIV*: For the flesh desires what is contrary to the Spirit, and the Spirit what is contrary to the flesh. They are in conflict with each other, so that you are not to do whatever you want. But if you are led by the Spirit, you are not under the law. The acts of the flesh are obvious: sexual immorality, impurity and debauchery; idolatry and witchcraft; hatred, discord, jealousy, fits of rage, selfish ambition, dissensions, factions, and envy; drunkenness, orgies, and the like. I warn you, as I did before, that those who live like this will not inherit the kingdom of God.*

As you can see, anger can cause acts of the flesh, which is contrary

49

to the Spirit of God. Dissensions are disagreements that lead to division. Does that sound familiar, sis? Hint, hint. God wants us to be slow to anger (**James 1:19 NIV**). He wants us to demonstrate the fruits of the Spirit vs the acts of the flesh. **Galatians 5:22-24 NIV:** But the fruit of the Spirit is love, joy, peace, forbearance, kindness, goodness, faithfulness, gentleness and self-control. Against such things there is no law. Those who belong to Christ Jesus have crucified the flesh with its passions and desires.

We have to crucify our own will, sis. Trust me, I know that isn't easy because oftentimes, we're in our id ego state and driven by our own desires. Living a life for Christ isn't easy. I try to remember that it wasn't easy for Christ to be crucified to remind myself of the ultimate sacrifice. He sacrificed for me, surely I can for Him, although I can't ever measure up. Listen, Diyah, I know we're all going to fall short, but honoring God's word, despite how challenging it is, leads to a far better outcome any day of the week than it does giving in to our flesh. **Ecclesiastes 7:9 KJV** states, be not hasty in thy spirit to be angry, for anger resteth in the bosom of fools. YOU'RE NOT A FOOL, DIYAH. Confess your sins to God each and every time. He is faithful and JUST to forgive you and cleanse you from all unrighteousness-**1 John 1:9 KJV**. You can rule over your anger. You can walk in the fruits of the Spirit. You can do all things through Christ who strengthens you-**Philippians 4:13 KJV**. But if you want to be forgiven, you must forgive. **Colossians 3:13 NIV** says Bear with each other and forgive one another if any of you has a grievance against someone. Forgive as the Lord forgave you. Forgiveness isn't for mom and dad, Diyah. It's for you to become unstuck, to live the life you want. The life you're living right now isn't God's design for you. The word says, He came to give you life more abundantly. Ask the Holy Spirit to help you resist the devil and to walk in your God ordained purpose.

If you want to discuss this further, let me know. Otherwise, I'm not going to mention it for a period of time because this must be your decision. I do pray God's word is received, that your heart is good soil, and that this takes root. Be encouraged. I love you. Shalom.

Sisterly,
Danita

Diyah yawned. She glances at the time on her cell phone. It was 5:18 PM. She still had plenty of time to rest before having to get to the bar that night for her shift. Jaylen and Sierra were both already sound asleep. She could hear them snoring. She checks to ensure her alarm is set, turns off the lamp on her nightstand, puts on her sleep mask, and slides underneath her covers. She feels Jaylen and Sierra adjust to her as she slides further into bed. *"Anger resteth in the bosom of fools. I've never heard that scripture before. I've never heard any preachers preach out of Ecclesiastes, that's why,"* Diyah thought to herself before she fell fast asleep.

She began to dream. *She was outside the gym, waiting for it to close. Her truck was parked across the street from the gym so it wouldn't be noticed. She knew by the absence of cars in the parking lot that Miguel was the only one left in the gym. She was waiting, crouched down behind his truck, dressed in all black. He drove a black 2023 Chevy Silverado. It took about 20 minutes after closing for him to come out. Her legs were burning with pain from crouching down for so long. She heard his footsteps approaching, getting closer and closer. Her heart raced faster and faster. She knew it was now or later. Right as Miguel hit his keyless remote to unlock his truck, she prepared herself...*

Knock. Knock. Knock. "Diyah Jones! Knightdale Police Department! We have a warrant to search your premises!" A voice called out to her from her dream. *Boom!* Diyah sat straight up in her bed. Jaylen and Sierra jumped down and ran underneath the bed. Her heart was racing, and she was breathing heavily. Detective Mills yelled again, "Diyah Jones! Knightdale Police Department! We have a warrant to search your premises!" She heard footsteps moving quickly. *Is this real?* She thought to herself. Then, before she knew it, she saw flashlights, and her bedroom ceiling light was turned on from the wall fixture. After her eyes adjusted to the light, she saw Detective Mills and another officer standing behind him, dressed in a standard-issued police uniform.

"What is going on? Why are y'all in my home?" Diyah demanded answers.

"We have a warrant to search your premises, Diyah. You're welcome to read it, but we're going to have to ask you to come into the living room and wait under officer surveillance while we search your home." Detective Mills instructed.

"I don't understand," Diyah said, confused.

"Officer, will you escort Ms. Jones to the living room, please and remain with her until we conduct the search?" Detective Mills instructed the officer behind him. The officer took the warrant from Detective Mills, handed it to Diyah, and motioned for her to walk to the living room with him. Diyah noticed that this officer resembled a younger, better-looking version of Barney Fife.

"We talked to Mr. Rivera, Diyah. He has reason to believe you assaulted him based on the confrontation you two had earlier Sunday evening. He said you even threatened him. We're going to search your home and your truck for any evidence. It's all in the warrant," Detective Mills informed Diyah while she was being escorted to the living room.

Diyah read the warrant and broke out into tears. She couldn't believe what was happening. She watched Detective Mills and the officers search for any evidence in her apartment. She knew they wouldn't find any evidence, but she was traumatized by it all. Her front door was busted in. She knew her neighbors were watching. She was so embarrassed. *How could Miguel do this to me? I can't believe this is happening to me,* she thought to herself. *God, please help me. I need you right now,"* she silently prayed. Just then, she saw Detective Mills coming down her hallway with a box in his hands.

"Diyah Jones, so you're the FC Attacker? You have the exact outfit that eyewitnesses have reported the FC Attacker wearing. Is that why you attacked Miguel? He has a daughter, Marisol, and a son, Adolfo, but I'm sure you know that because you only attack fathers."

"What? No! I'm not the FC Attacker! I can expl.." Diyah attempted to defend herself.

"Diyah Jones, you're under arrest for the aggravated assault and battery on Pernell Williams, Cleveland Phillips, Lee Brown, Arthur Washington, and lastly Miguel Sánchez Rivera. You have the right to remain silent; anything you say can and will be used against you in a court of law. You have the right to an attorney. If you cannot afford an attorney, one will be provided for you," Detective Mills read Diyah her Miranda Rights while the officer handcuffed her hands behind her back. Diyah continued to cry as the officer escorted her out of her apartment. He didn't even bother to throw a coat over her shoulders. She couldn't believe this was happening to her.

"Wait!" Diyah stopped walking abruptly. "I have two cats inside. They're in my bedroom. Please shut the bedroom door so they cannot get out of the apartment. My front door is busted. PLEASE!" She pleaded with Detective Mills, still crying.

Detective Mills glared at Diyah for a moment. "Fine, I'll make sure my officers secure the cats until someone can come get them. They're still underneath the bed. We saw them while we were searching. Now, keep walking before I change my mind."

"Thank you," Diyah responded and resumed walking down her breezeway towards the stairs as the officer guided her. She thought to herself, *Rah told me to get rid of those clothes, but I hadn't thought about it anymore.* At that moment, Diyah remembered something else too: *be not hasty in thy spirit to be angry, for anger resteth in the bosom of fools.* At this moment, Diyah felt like a big ol' fool.

Chapter 8
A Daughter Never Outgrows the Heart

Ring. Ring. Ring. Ring. Dawson stirs from his sleep. He realizes that he'd fallen asleep in his La-Z-Boy recliner again while watching TV. Dawson Jones was a 71-year-old Hershey Chocolate man with a muscular physique. He stood 6'7" and 240lbs. He wore his pepper/salt mixed hair in a short fade with waves, and he had a pepper/salt Van Dyke goatee. *Ring. Ring.* Dawson looks up at his wall clock in front of him and sees it's 10:45 PM. He had not prepared for bed, so he was still wearing a long-sleeved burgundy Hanes heavyweight shirt, relaxed-fit mid-washed carpenter jeans, and a pair of white and gray crew socks. His cell phone was resting on the single, wooden, black folding tray table sitting to his right. He picks up his cell phone and notices the caller ID says No Caller ID. He felt urged to answer. He clears his throat from his slumber. "Hello," Dawson answers.

"Hello, this is a prepaid collect call from Diyah Jones, an inmate in Wake County Detention Center. This call is subject to recording and monitoring. To accept charges, press 1, to refuse charges, press 2," the automated recording stated. Dawson pressed 1. "Thank you, you may start the conversation now," the automated recording concluded.

"Daddy, daddy, thank God you answered. Daddy, I'm in trouble," Diyah began to sob.

"Diyah sweetie, what's going on? Why are you calling me from jail? Are you ok?" Dawson questioned with a trembling voice.

"Daddy, they think I'm the FC Attacker," Diyah continued to sob.

"The man from the news! I don't understand. Diyah, what's going on? Are you ok, Diyah?" Dawson continued to question.

"Daddy, I don't have much time to talk, but I'm innocent! I'm innocent, daddy! And, yes, physically I'm ok. Can you get me a lawyer? Can you get me out of here? I gotta get out of here, daddy! Please!" Diyah pleaded through her sobs.

"I'll get you a lawyer, Diyah, but sweetheart, it's the night before Thanksgiving. I don't know how quickly you'll be released. It'll take a miracle, honey." Diyah continued to sob. "Diyah, sweetie? It's gonna be ok. I promise. It's gonna be ok. Daddy's got you. I just need some time," Dawson attempted to soothe Diyah.

"Thank you, daddy. And, can someone go to my apartment, get Jaylen and Sierra, and take care of them until I'm released? I know y'all have never been to my new place, but you send gifts, so I assume you know where I live now."

"Yes, we know exactly where you live, Diyah. I'll make sure everything is taken care of," Dawson reassured her. "But, I don't understand. How could they arrest you? What evidence do they have?"

"They found something in my home, but it's a misunderstanding. Miguel was attacked, and he told the police he thinks it was me."

"Miguel?" Dawson asked with confusion.

Diyah paused before answering. "My biological father."

"Oh," Dawson said with surprise.

"It's a big misunderstanding, Daddy. I promise," Diyah tried to sound convincing.

"I trust God, Diyah. Everything will be ok," Dawson encouraged himself and Diyah.

"I'm sorry, daddy, this is all my fault," Diyah said between tears.

"How is this your fault? I thought you said you were innocent?" Dawson asked.

56

"Daddy, I got 30 more seconds on this call. I am innocent. I'll call back when I can. Don't forget Jaylen and Sierra. Thank you, daddy. I love you."

"Make sure you pray, Diyah, you know God. I'll be praying for you, and we all will. I'll get right on everything. I love you, too, baby girl. Keep the faith and watch your back, you hear?" *Click.* "Diyah! Diyah, do you hear me?" Dawson asked, but the only response he received was the dial tone. Dawson took a deep breath, he kneeled at his La-Z-Boy recliner, and prayed. "Lord, I come to you in the precious name of Jesus. I ask that you give me strength and be with Diyah right now. Let your rod and staff comfort her. Give her strength. Dispatch Angels around her to protect her. May her Angels fight on her behalf. Provide a way of escape from this situation, Lord. Help her to bear. Manifest the right lawyer for her. Be with this entire family as we navigate this test, ordain our steps. We need you now to be Jehovah-Nissi and Jehovah-Shalom. I trust your word, all things work together for good to those that love God, to those who are called according to His purpose. Use this situation for your glory, Lord. Draw Diyah back to you and this family closer together. I pray that she has a repentant heart. Thank you for your faithfulness. I know your compassions never fail. I count it done in faith. In Jesus' name. Amen." Once he arose, he realized that he'd started to cry at some point. He blew his nose with a paper towel he had sitting on his single folding tray table. He took a few more deep breaths, and then he dialed Daisy, Diyah's mother.

Daisy Jones was a 66-year-old woman with a russet brown complexion who stood 5'7". She had freckles on her cheekbones, full lips, and black curly, kinky, thick hair that she had twisted up underneath her black satin bonnet. Daisy was sound asleep, lying in her Queen Posturepedic bed, when she was awakened by a noise. *Ring. Ring. Ring.* Daisy looks at the caller ID. She sees it's Dawson's number. She sits up in the bed and picks up the phone with urgency. "Dawson, is everything ok?" She asks with a husky voice.

"No, Daisy. It's Diyah-"

"What's the matter with Diyah?" Daisy asks, cutting Dawson off.

"She's locked up."

"What? Why is she locked up?"

"Let me explain. They think she's the FC Attacker. They found something in her home. She didn't say what, but it led them to believe she's the FC Attacker because Miguel said she attacked him. She says she's innocent of it all." Daisy became quiet. "Daisy, you there?"

"Yes, Dawson, I'm here. I'm just processing everything. So they've met?"

"Apparently. I didn't ask the specifics. She needs a lawyer. She wants to be released until the trial. I don't know what we can do with Thanksgiving being tomorrow."

"Oh God, you're right! Dawson, what are we going to do?" Daisy began to cry. "I don't want anything to happen to her while she's in there."

"It'll be all right, Daisy. I've already prayed. We're going to do what we can, but it may not be much physically within our power until next week.

"Did she say she was ok? How did she sound?" Daisy asked between sobs.

"She said physically she was fine. She is scared. She was crying. She did ask for someone to go over and get Jaylen and Sierra." Daisy became quiet again. "Daisy?"

"I'm sorry, Dawson. You're going to go get the cats, right?"

Dawson observed that Daisy seemed to have stopped crying. "Yes, I'll go as soon as we hang up."

"I think there's a well-known criminal lawyer who attends Danita's church. I'll call and ask her. That lawyer may help us out before Monday. What did they charge her with?"

"I didn't even ask, but if they think she's the FC Attacker, this is serious. Those reports of each attack have been all over the news."

"Yeah, this is serious, but God is able. Anything else I should know? What jail is she in?"

"Wake County Detention Center," Dawson answered.

"Ok, be safe going over to her apartment, Dawson. You know that's not the best neighborhood. Call me when you get back in. I'll be up praying."

"I will."

"Ok, I'm going to call Danita now. I hate to disturb her, considering her grief has caused sleep disruptions already."

"She'd want you to call her," Dawson reassured Daisy. "Let me get off this phone, it'll be 12 soon."

"Ok, talk to you later."

"Ok," Dawson responded.

Daisy sat in her thoughts for a few minutes. She couldn't believe that her youngest daughter was not only locked up, but also accused of being the FC Attacker. She was also curious about how long she and Miguel had been interacting. Daisy's heart ached. A year had passed since she'd spoken to Diyah. Daisy hadn't said this to Dawson, but she wondered what made Diyah call Dawson instead of her, considering Dawson and Diyah's strained relationship throughout the years. *She must still be upset with me more so than Dawson,* Daisy thought to herself. *Focus, Daisy,* she redirected her thoughts. Just then, Daisy climbed out of bed, knelt on her red embroidered "The Lord is my Shepherd" cushioned kneeling pad and prayed before calling Danita.

Forty-five minutes later, Dawson was standing at Diyah's door. He observed that the door was pulled to, but it wasn't secure; anyone could push on it, and it would open. He'd already called Cyclone Doors, a 24/7 door repair service in Knightdale, to meet him at Diyah's apartment and repair her door. He stepped inside. The place was surprisingly neat considering the police had searched it. Dawson assumed this was partly due to Diyah's simplistic lifestyle. He took a look around. This was his first time in Diyah's home.

Aside from a few hours ago, he had not spoken to her in a year. She'd not let him or Daisy know when she moved, but Danita kept them in the loop. He observed the layout: brown carpet in the tiny living room, which consisted of her dark teal faux leather couch & greyish teal wooden chair side end table, both from her old place, a cat scratching post, and a litter box in the corner. He observed the small kitchen, the pantry, and the lack of seating for dining. Dawson was surprised that Diyah's 32" flatscreen TV was still mounted on the beige wall, considering the neighborhood and the door not being secured after the police left. He continued on down the hall, using the brown carpet as his guide. He noticed the bathroom was on the left. He fumbled around the wall until he found the light and clicked it on. It was a full bath. It had the same beige walls as the living room, a white sink, a small white vanity, a white toilet, a white bathtub, and a white porcelain square tile floor. He took note that Diyah had no decorations, just a gray shower curtain with a black Sphinx cat and caption-"let's get naked", and a black memory foam floor mat in front of the tub. He turned off the light and was about to continue to Diyah's bedroom when he heard a knock.

"Cyclone Doors! I'm looking for Mr. Dawson Jones," a man called out from the front of the apartment.

"Yes, I'm here," Dawson responded, walking back into the living room. He extended his hand to the technician once arriving at the door. He was Caucasian, stood about 5'11", of a middle build, with brown eyes, and brown hair that was covered by his Cyclone Doors cap. He wore a white polo shirt from Cyclone Doors, which was tucked into his dark denim jeans. "I'm Dawson Jones."

"I'm Ronnie Price," he responded, shaking Dawson's hand.

"I'm sure glad you guys answer calls at this hour, especially considering the Holiday. Like I mentioned on the phone, I need a door and door frame replaced," Dawson stated, pointing to the door.

"Glad to be at your service, Mr. Dawson, but has the landlord authorized this?"

"Yes, I've spoken with them. I'll make sure their master is re-keyed to fit this door. They are appreciative that I'm taking care of all of this to be honest, so they couldn't care less."

"Ok, well, I'll get right to it."

"Thanks, I'll be in the back, just holler if you need me". Dawson detoured back towards the bedroom. He was sure Jaylen and Sierra were hungry. He opened Diyah's bedroom door and fumbled around for the light. He saw Diyah's full-sized bed unmade in front of him. He looked around and noticed a Mahogany 6 drawer dresser with a mirror, a matching Mahogany 5 drawer Chester dresser, and another litter box. "Jaylen? Sierra? Come to grandpop." It had been a year since Dawson had seen the cats. He listened for a sound, but didn't hear any. *They're probably scared*, he thought to himself. He got down on all fours so he could look underneath the bed. He used the light from his cell to get additional lighting. "There go grandpop's babies", he said to them. Dawson extended his hand underneath the bed so they could smell his scent. Jaylen backed up, but Sierra sniffed his hand. "I know what y'all want. Let me get you some food," Dawson began to search for food. He saw their food bowls. When he could not find any food, he then figured that Diyah most likely kept their food in the kitchen.

A minute later, Dawson returned to the bedroom after finding their food in the pantry. He had 2 servings of Iams Perfect Portions Salmon Recipe. He scooped a serving apiece in each bowl with a spoon. Jaylen and Sierra slowly peeked out from underneath the bed to the sound and smell of Salmon. They each looked at him and then at their bowls. "It's ok, babies," he said to soothe them. He dumped some chicken-flavored True Chews by Blue Buffalo on the floor, creating a trail leading up to their respective bowls to encourage them to come eat. Dawson left the room, shutting the bedroom door behind him while Ronnie worked, so he could start gathering their carriers, food, and litter to take them home.

An hour later, Dawson had paid and tipped Ronnie, locked up, and secured Jaylen and Sierra in the back seat of his 2021 White Toyota Tacoma truck, along with their food, toys, a shared bed, their scratching post, and litter. He also found Diyah's debit and credit cards and took them along with her driver's license, social security card, and birth certificate. He just didn't trust leaving those items, knowing the type of neighborhood she lived in and that the neighborhood was aware she had been arrested, which made her apartment vulnerable. It was nearly 3 in the morning when Dawson returned, got himself and the cats settled, before he was able to call Daisy. She answered immediately.

"Hello, everything ok, Dawson? That took longer than I expected," Daisy answered.

"Yes, everything is fine. I got the door replaced while I was there, and her cards. I wanted the apartment to be as secure as possible until she returns."

"Oh, I didn't think of that," Daisy responded. She paused. "Thank you, Dawson. You're such a good father," Daisy expressed, fighting back tears while thinking about how Dawson was there despite the past.

"No thanks needed. That's my baby girl. She's never left my heart," Dawson said, choking back emotions himself.

"I know. I'll see you at Danita's in a few hours. She was devastated, but Amir had her. She wouldn't call the lawyer this time of night, but she will later on in the morning. Try to get some rest."

"Thanks for the update. You try to get some rest, too. Good night, Daisy."

Chapter 9
In Everything Give Thanks
Part 1

Diyah awakes to a trickling sound of water. She opens her eyes and takes in her surroundings. It took her a few seconds to remember that she had been arrested and that she was currently incarcerated. She realizes she must have finally fallen asleep from exhaustion. Her cellmate, Amy, was using the bathroom right next to her bunk. Since she was the fresh fish, she had the pleasure of sleeping on the bottom bunk. *BRAAARPT!* Diyah immediately turns over to face the wall away from Amy. Diyah could tell by the smell that Amy was doing more than peeing. Amy was a Caucasian female who was 18 years old. She stood about 5'2", slim build, with blonde hair and green eyes. Amy had taken a liking to Diyah. She was eager to have someone to talk to because she loved to talk and laugh. Amy had aged out of foster care and opted not to transition to the 18-21 program. Amy shared that she'd been kicked out of her boyfriend's home and had been caught stealing money to buy food. Amy was hoping her life's story would evoke sympathy at her upcoming trial, especially since this was her first offense. It was Amy's plan to see if she could still transition into the 18-21 program. Amy also gave Diyah an overview of the prison, including the schedule, the guards, and provided descriptions of everyone on their cell block. Diyah was thankful for Amy; however, she still had her guard up. Diyah planned to watch Amy along with everyone else. Rumors had spread that Diyah was the FC Attacker, which meant some might test her to prove a point, while others would fear her. Therefore, it was imperative for her to remain hypervigilant. As far as she was concerned, no one was to be trusted, but she would stick close to Amy for now.

"Happy Thanksgiving, fish," Amy said as she'd just finished wiping her butt and washing her hands.

"What's there to be thankful about?" Diyah questioned.

"I'm not on the street, I'm not cold, and we will have a special lunch and dinner since it's Thanksgiving. You'll see," Amy responded as she was climbing up to her bunk. "What do you have to be thankful for?" Diyah thought about Amy's question for a few minutes. She didn't think she had anything to be thankful for. Her life was a mess. She blamed her mom. *If only she'd told me the truth as a child*, she thought to herself. "Earth to fish! You asleep?" Amy questioned, interrupting Diyah's thoughts.

"No, I'm not asleep. I was thinking about your question," Diyah responded.

"Well, what are you thankful for?" Amy pressed.

"I don't have anything to be thankful for," Diyah finally responded.

"Yeah, you do. There's always something to be thankful for. My grandmother, God rest her soul, would often say, "in everything, give thanks". I know it's a scripture, but I don't know where it is in the Bible."

"That's first **Thessalonians 5:18**," Diyah informed Amy.

"How do you know that?" Amy asked with curiosity.

"I grew up in the church. Sunday school, children's meditation, Vacation Bible School, church every Sunday, Bible Study on Wednesdays, that was my childhood," Diyah explained.

"Sounds like you had a good childhood. I had a good childhood, too, until my grandmother died. My religion died with her." Amy paused. "What went wrong for you, church girl? What led the church girl to grow up and start attacking fathers?" Amy giggled.

"I don't want to talk about it," Diyah responded. "And, I told you that I'm innocent."

"Yeah, so is everyone in here," Amy chuckled. "Tell me what you're thankful for," Amy wouldn't let up. "I'm not going to stop asking."

Diyah thought for a few minutes. "If I tell you, will you let me go to sleep?" Diyah asked.

"Yeah, fish, I'll let you go to sleep, but it better be something genuine. My grandmother used to make us go around the table and say what we were thankful for on Thanksgiving. So, what are you thankful for?"

Diyah paused. "I'm thankful for my sister. I'm thankful that Dawson answered the phone when I called him last night, and that he is willing to help me. That's it."

"Who's Dawson?" Amy asked.

"Nope, I answered your question. I'm going to sleep," Diyah responded firmly.

"Okaay," Amy whined. "Go to sleep, fish. You have a couple of hours before showers and chow time anyways."

Diyah tried to get comfortable; however, now that there was silence, the lingering smell from Amy's bowel was all she could focus on. It smelled like sewage. Diyah attempted to distract herself, and she began thinking about Jaylen and Sierra. She wasn't used to sleeping without them, and her heart began to ache. She knew they were wondering where she was. She hoped that Dawson didn't wait to go see about them because she'd called him late last night. *Why would he rush to go see about them? You hadn't spoken to him in a year,* she thought to herself. Diyah began to cry silently. She hoped that Amy wouldn't hear her because that would start another conversation. Diyah continued to cry until exhaustion welcomed her back to sleep.

A couple of hours later, Diyah awoke to the sounds from her environment. She heard dialogue and movement from the cell block. She saw Amy standing in front of their bunks. "Wake up, fish, if you're trying to shower before chow," Amy instructed her. Diyah's heart began to race. She desperately wanted a shower, but she did not know what to expect. This would be her first shower since being detained. She wasn't shy about her body, but being naked in a shower with other women could pose a threat, although the guards were supposed to observe the shower time. "Come on, grab your things," Amy coached her. Diyah silently prayed, *Lord, I need you to be with me and go before me. Protect me every second of my days here. I know you are with me, and you are my God. In Jesus name, Amen.*

"Fish, do you hear me?" Amy asked.

"Yeah, I was just praying. I'm getting up." Diyah responded as she sat up.

Amy giggled, "You found some other things to thank the man upstairs for?"

"Yeah, something like that," Diyah responded as she began to mimic Amy. She gathered a clean facility-issued uniform consisting of an orange top and matching pants, and clean white underwear. She slipped into her facility-issued shower shoes, and she grabbed her soap.

"Don't drop your soap," Amy giggled. Diyah froze, and Amy read her mind. "You don't have that to worry about, fish, but the floors are nasty, you don't want to drop your soap." Diyah took a deep breath. "You gotta toughen up, though, fish. Your eyes are puffy, I assume from crying. Don't make yourself a target more so than you already are," Amy continued to giggle.

Diyah took another deep breath and put on a brave stance. She gave Amy a look that could kill, which made Amy stop her giggling abruptly. What Amy didn't know was that Diyah was an excellent fighter. She's had to square up countless nights at parties. And even if she was outnumbered, she knew how to put on a brave face. "Is this tough enough for you?" Diyah gave Amy a smug smile, "Let's go." Diyah motioned for Amy to lead the way.

Chapter 10
In Everything Give Thanks
Part 2

It's Thanksgiving Day, Danita reminds herself as she awakens from her sleep. She looks over at her clock. It was 6:50 AM. She looked over at Amir, using the sunlight that was peeping through their curtains. She notices that he is still sound asleep. He'd stayed up with her most of the night. Initially, she was up because of the grief of the miscarriage, but after receiving the news about Diyah from her mom, falling asleep became even more of a challenge. After receiving the news, they decided to use the time left to clean up and prepare for their guest today. Both Amir's family and Danita's family will be joining them for Thanksgiving today. Normally, they'd have three separate Thanksgiving celebrations: brunch with the Franklins, Thanksgiving afternoon game with Dawson, and Thanksgiving dinner with Daisy. But considering the circumstances, it was agreed that everyone would come together to celebrate this year. Danita was even more appreciative because the little strength she'd gained over the past 3 weeks seemed to have left her after learning about Diyah. She did not feel like celebrating. She couldn't believe her sister was locked up. *Is she really the FC Attacker?* She thought to herself.

Danita picks up her cell phone and reads the verse of the day from her Bible App. It was 1 Thessalonians 5:18. Danita decided to read the entire chapter. She felt somewhat encouraged after reading the chapter, particularly verses 16-18: "16-rejoice evermore. 17-Pray without ceasing. 18-In every thing give thanks: for this is the will of God in Christ Jesus concerning you." Danita slowly climbs out of their king-sized bed because she didn't want to disturb Amir. She planned to go to the office to give thanks and pray for Diyah and the family's strength to endure this Thanksgiving Holiday.

Four hours later, Danita had prayed, cried, prayed again, and read some more scripture. She watched the news and learned that

Diyah was the morning's breaking news. She was so embarrassed for Diyah and the family. Thankfully, she'd had a light breakfast before watching the news. Once she was able to calm herself, she cooked a green bean casserole, a sweet potato casserole, and made 2 pecan pies. Afterwards, she cleaned up the kitchen, showered, and dressed. She was currently wearing a navy blue, casual short-sleeve shirt that matched her wide-leg navy blue linen pants, and a pair of gray Dearfoams house slippers. She had the front of her shirt tucked into her pants to give the illusion of a flatter stomach. Her hair was styled in big box braids, which she then pulled up into a bun. Amir had offered to help her in the kitchen; however, she wanted time to be alone and keep busy. Amir was dressed in a Nike Jared Goff Blue Detroit Lions Game Jersey, dark denim Wrangler jeans and black ankle socks. She overheard the football game coming from the living room, which had started about half an hour ago. The Green Bay Packers were playing the Detroit Lions. *Ding Dong. That must be momma or Pop William and Ma Belle,* Danita thought to herself as she hung her dish rag across the sink.

"I'll get it!" Amir called out from the living room. She was surprised he pulled himself out of the game while his team was playing. A few seconds later, she heard him say, "Hey, Ma Daisy. Happy Thanksgiving! How are you holding up?" Daisy was wearing a camel double-breasted peacoat over a burgundy lightweight crew-neck button sweater, which exposed a white shirt underneath, tucked into her maple taffy wide-leg relaxed-fit trousers, and a pair of dark brown Clarks.

"Hey Amir, I'm trusting in the Lord. That's all I can do, you know?"

"I understand that. Here, let me take your coat and those bags," Amir offered.

"Thank you. Amir! Son, what have you done to your hair?"

Amir rubbed his sharp drop fade haircut. "It felt heavy recently, you know? It may seem small, but it became too much. Once I really opened up to Danita about how the miscarriage was impacting me, I got the desire to cut it low." Amir offered an uncomfortable smile.

"I understand, son. I am just shocked to see you with so little hair. It looks good on you. It makes you look younger. Come here and give me a proper hug," Daisy comforted him.

Danita came up behind Amir and overheard the last part of their conversation. "Hey, ma. Your twist out looks great!" Danita hugged her mother after she'd released Amir.

"Hey, baby, thanks," Daisy responded, rubbing Danita's back while embracing her. "It smells good in here. What are you cooking?"

"I made a green bean casserole, sweet potato casserole, and pecan pies," Danita responded.

"That sounds good. So how are you?" Daisy asked.

"I'm confused, ma. I have so many questions about Diyah's arrest. Then the news this morning. I have so many emotions. I'm exhausted, but I shifted into task mode. I've been keeping busy since last night and this morning. How about you?"

"Like I told Amir, I'm trusting in the Lord. The news broadcast was a shocker, though, I must say," Daisy expressed with a weak voice. The three of them were walking into the kitchen.

Amir sat Daisy's bags on the butcher-blocked island, and Danita and Daisy sat down at the island next to each other. "You ladies need me to do anything?" He asked.

"No, bae, we're good," Danita smiled at Amir. "You can return to your game, I know you want to." Amir kissed Danita on the cheek before exiting the kitchen. Turning to her mother, she asked, "So what do you need me to do, ma?"

"Nothing, baby. I've already pre-mixed the dressing. I'll put that in the oven later so it'll be hot when we're ready to eat. Everything else is done aside from the gravy. I'll make that later, too. I thought we could chat before everyone else arrives," Daisy suggested. "Have you contacted the lawyer yet from your church? What's her name?"

"Constance Shaw and I have. She didn't answer, so I left a voicemail. I don't know if she's out of town for the Holiday or just busy with the morning prep like the rest of us."

"Oh, that's disappointing news. I'm just so worried about Diyah.

God knows what kind of people she's in there with. I just wish we had heard from her by now. Dawson said he would add me to the call the next time she contacts him. You haven't heard from her, right?" Daisy asked.

"No ma, I haven't, but I'll do the same if I do hear from her. I'm sure Diyah is safe. She's a survivor," Danita reached over and squeezed her mother's hand. "Ma, I can't help but wonder if Diyah is really the FC Attacker."

"Danita! How could you think that about your sister?" Daisy scolded and gave Danita a stern look. "Of course she's innocent."

"Maybe she's not the FC Attacker, but none of us really knows the present-day Diyah. I mean, why would Miguel think she attacked him? I didn't even know they'd met. And the police found some kind of evidence in her home? Ma, we have to prepare ourselves that Diyah might be guilty of at least attacking Miguel," Danita pleaded.

"Danita Jones Franklin. I cannot believe you would even consider any of these theories about Diyah. She is your sister, for God's sake!" Daisy shook her head in disappointment.

"Yes, she is my sister, and I know she's always had a temper, but this news about daddy not being her biological father changed her. It hurt her deeply. There are too many red flags about all of this. She was here on Monday and admitted she was angry. She looked convicted when we were talking about doing something out of anger that you'd later regret. I didn't pay attention to it in the moment, but since hearing about her arrest, I've been reflecting on our dialogue," Danita explained. "I don't want my thoughts to be true. I'm just anxious."

"I see," Daisy responded. "I guess I hadn't considered the possibility she could be guilty, and I don't want to consider it now. I carried that child for 40 weeks; I know her. She couldn't have attacked Miguel, and surely she isn't the FC Attacker. I must admit that it was a genuine surprise to learn that she and Miguel had met. I, too, wonder about why he would accuse her. I've been thinking about reaching out to him. I don't know if he'd see me. I don't know if it's a good idea to even speak to him, considering it was his accusation that started all of this," Daisy shared her thoughts.

She'd begun to tear up.

"Contacting him is tempting, maybe it's best we wait to see what Constance says?" Danita suggested handing Daisy a napkin.

"I hope Diyah calls soon," Daisy whimpered. "I just want to hear her voice."

"Me too," Danita responded.

"How are you doing otherwise, with the miscarriage, I mean?" Daisy turned her attention to Danita.

"I am better. I'm not crying as much. But I still have trouble sleeping. I shared with Diyah that I experience anger at times in addition to sadness. Guilt at times; I was feeling lonely until Amir truly opened up to me," Danita disclosed. "I have moments when I'm fine, but this doesn't help. I felt like I was just getting my sister back, and that was a comfort, but suppose this goes badly, ma? Suppose she goes away for a long time? That'll be another loss," Danita began to cry.

Daisy pulled Danita into her arms. "Do I need to go get Amir?" Daisy asked Danita as she was holding her tightly. Danita shook her head no. In that moment, she needed to be in her mother's arms. Daisy rubbed Danita's back, "Let it out, sweetie. This is scary, I know, but we must trust God. He will use this for Diyah's benefit and His glory. We must believe." Danita began to settle down.

"Thanks, ma. I know you're right, but it is a challenge keeping the faith. I'm going to go wash my face," Danita said as she let go of her mother. *Ding dong.*

"I'll get the door, go on and wash your face," Daisy offered.

"Y'all want me to get that?" Amir called out from the living room. He was glued to the TV screen.

"No, son, I'll get it," Daisy called back as Danita headed towards her en-suite. Daisy headed towards the door and saw, through the fiberglass, to her surprise, that it was Dawson, William, and Belle. "Hey y'all. Come on in. Happy Thanksgiving," Daisy greeted everyone as she opened the door.

"Hey, Daisy. Happy Thanksgiving," Dawson stepped into the entryway first, hugged Daisy, and began to take off his coat. He was wearing a walnut-brown, long-sleeved button-up shirt tucked into his creased, navy-blue, slim-fit chino pants and brown leather shoes.

"Hey, Daisy! Happy Thanksgiving. How are you?" Belle asked, hugging Daisy. Maybelle "Belle" Franklin was Amir's mother. She was a peanut brown complexioned woman who was 71 years old, stood 5'5", and had gray locs that were pulled back into a ponytail.

"I'm trusting in the Lord," Daisy responded. "How are y'all?" Daisy asked, looking back and forth from Belle to William. She was secretly hoping that William and Belle had not seen the news that morning, but she knew deep down they had.

"We're just fine," William answered for himself and his wife. It was now William's turn to hug Daisy. William Franklin was Amir's father. He was 73 years old, stood 6'5", had a red-brown complexion, and a bald head.

"We've been praying for everyone," Belle offered. William helped Belle remove her coat, and then he took off his. Belle was wearing a knee-length tan sweater dress with an espresso-brown scarf tied in a Parisian knot, black leggings, and dark-brown leather Clark ankle boots. Belle untied her scarf and handed it to William, who hung it on the coat rack in the entryway. William was wearing an olive green turtleneck, a pair of St. John's Bay slim-fit beige chinos, and a pair of dark brown St. John's Bay Rutland flat-heeled boots.

"Thanks, the prayers are needed," Daisy responded.

"Amen to that," Dawson chimed in.

"How are the kids?" Belle inquired; however, Dawson and William were pondering the same question, little did Belle know.

"Danita feels like this situation with Diyah is a setback to her healing journey. Amir, well, he seems to be coming along. Have you seen his hair?" Daisy asked.

"No," William and Belle responded.

"Danita! Amir! Everyone's here!" Daisy called out.

"I'm here," Amir stated, coming down the hall. "I was wondering who it was. Happy Thanksgiving." He smiled, looking at his family. He hugged his mother first. "Hey, ma."

"Hey, son. I love the new look," Belle complimented Amir. She was secretly thankful that Daisy warned her, so she didn't appear shocked.

"Do you like it really?" Amir asked earnestly.

"Yes, I truly do. I haven't seen you wear that cut in years. You wear it well."

"Thanks, ma," Amir responded. He then shook his father's and father-in-law's hands as he embraced them both. He said to the men, "The game is on. The Packers are in the lead right now. Come on into the living room."

"Not before I get my hugs," Danita appeared and interjected. "Happy Thanksgiving, everyone!" She hugged her father first, Ma Belle, and then Pop Dawson.

"How are you?" Dawson asked.

"I'm doing the best I can, daddy. How are the cats?" Danita asked.

"They're fine. They had duck canned food for breakfast, and I'll make sure they have homestyle turkey casserole canned food for dinner," Dawson responded. "I'm here for you, Danita. We're all here for you and Amir," Dawson said, grabbing Danita's hand.

"I know you are daddy. I know you all are," Danita looked around to her family.

"We appreciate that, Pop Dawson. We appreciate the support from all of you," Amir offered.

"Well, since we're all here, let's finish off the meal. We can eat sooner," Belle suggested, and everyone agreed.

An hour and a half later, everyone was seated at the 8-seater, solid wooden, light-brown dining room table for Thanksgiving lunch. The home was filled with harmonious notes of celery and onion, complemented by subtle sweet notes of cinnamon, nutmeg, and caramelized sugar. Amir was sitting at the head of the table, and Danita was sitting opposite him at the other end of the table. William and Belle were sitting side by side to Amir's right, and Dawson and Daisy were sitting on Amir's left; however, they had an empty chair between them. They had turkey, dressing, gravy, roast beef, and potatoes, as well as green bean casserole, turnip greens, deviled eggs, sweet potato casserole, baked mac n cheese, and pecan pie and carrot cake for dessert. Amir's team, the Detroit Lions, lost. The final score was 29-22 in the Packers' favor. The lawyer, Constance Shaw, had still not returned Danita's phone call, nor had anyone heard from Diyah.

"Everyone ready for grace?" Amir asked. Everyone nodded in agreement and began to reach for each other's hands. "Lord, we thank you for this day. We thank you for this great family. We thank you for the mobility of our limbs, normal bodily functions, and that we're enclosed in our right minds. We thank you for all the provisions. We thank you for being omnipresent, and you're in the midst of the Franklin and Jones families. We thank you for working things out on Diyah's behalf. Thank you for keeping her safe, Lord God. Continue to keep your angels around her. We thank you for this food. Lord, we ask that you touch each family member of the Franklin and Jones families today, whether they are here at this table or somewhere else. Heal us emotionally, let us feel your presence as we continue to draw nearer to thee. We accept the peace freely given to us from the finished work at the cross. We turn to you so that our mourning will be turned into dancing. You have removed our sackcloths and girded us with gladness. We will give you thanks for ever. Bless this food so that it may be nutritious to our bodies and nourishment to our health. Bless the hands that prepared it. In Jesus' name we pray, in faith, amen."

"Amen," everyone said in unison.

"Beautiful prayer, son," Belle complimented. "Was that Psalms 30 you referenced?"

"Yes, ma'am," Amir responded as he had begun carving the golden brown turkey and handing out portions.

"Belle, I understand that Isaiah is having Thanksgiving with his girlfriend and her family?" Daisy asked as they were passing dishes around to plate. Isaiah Franklin was Amir's older brother. He was 35 years old, stood 6'5" like his father and brother, shared his mother's peanut brown complexion, slim build, and had locs.

"Yes, he is. It seems to be getting serious," Belle commented.

"Have y'all met her? What's her name?" Daisy asked.

"Dené, and no, we haven't. They're supposed to celebrate Christmas with us. I'm looking forward to that," Belle admitted. "It doesn't feel right not having him here."

"Do they live close?" Daisy asked.

"No, her grandmother lives in Moyock and that's where they go for Thanksgiving," Belle responded.

"What's that near?" Danita asked.

"It's up around Elizabeth City," William answered.

"Oh, that's about a 2-hour drive one way, so unfortunately, Isaiah couldn't swing both families for the Holidays," Daisy observed.

"No, unfortunately, he can't," Belle complained.

"Dear?" William spoke. "If this young lady is the one, this is something we have to accept. The word says a man shall leave his father and mother, and cleave to his wife."

"I know, I know," Belle responded. "It'll just take some time getting used to it, that's all."

"I understand," William empathized.

"I understand, too," Daisy offered. "As the family grows, it can be harder to keep everyone connected. I know Isaiah will make sure you all will be included," Daisy attempted to comfort Belle.

"Thank you," Belle expressed her gratitude.

"Ma, you still have your favorite son here?" Amir joked. He was also attempting to comfort his mother.

"I have no favorites, you know that," Belle said, smiling at Amir. "But I am thankful to be able to spend Thanksgiving with you this year.

Silence fell over the room for the next thirty minutes as everyone enjoyed their plates and returned for seconds. The only words spoken were to compliment everyone's favorite dish they were enjoying. *Ring. Ring.* All eyes fell on Dawson. He, Daisy, and Danita were hoping that Diyah would call. Daisy felt the weight of her heart in her stomach. Dawson began wiping his hands so he could pull his phone out of its clip. *Ring. Ring.* The caller ID read No Caller ID. Dawson answered, putting the phone on the table, and enabled the speaker. He hit 1 and accepted the charges when the automated voice prompted him.

"Diyah sweetie," Dawson called out. "I'm here with everyone at Amir's and Danita's. You're on speaker. Your mom is here, Danita, Amir, and his parents. Are you there, sweetie?"

"Hey, daddy, yes, I'm here. Hey everybody," Diyah sounded emotional, but she was trying to sound strong. "Happy Thanksgiving. How are Jaylen and Sierra?"

"They're just fine, sweetie. They're at my house. They're eating good, and they have their bed and clawing post. I'm making sure they're well taken care of. I secured your apartment as well."

"I can't thank you enough, daddy," Diyah expressed.

"Baby, this is momma. How are you holding up?" Daisy asked.

"I'm ok physically," Diyah responded.

"Have you eaten?" Daisy asked.

"Yes, they served us turkey, mashed potatoes with gravy, string beans, and a dinner roll. We had pumpkin pie," Diyah answered.

"I'm praying for you, Diyah," Daisy informed her.

"We all are," Danita chimed in. "I called my church member who's a lawyer, but she hasn't returned my call yet. I'll call again tomorrow if she hasn't called me."

"I gotta get out of here, sis," Diyah's voice cracked as she pleaded.

"Just hold on, baby," Dawson responded. "We're doing the best we can, considering the Holiday. We'll be able to do more next week. We'll contact more lawyers if we have to."

"Thanks, daddy," Diyah said.

"We miss you, Diyah. It's not the same without you," Daisy expressed.

"No, things are not the same," Diyah highlighted. Daisy and everyone else took note of what Diyah didn't say in response to Daisy's affection. Silence.

Dawson cleared his throat, "Diyah, you make sure you say your prayers and keep the faith. God hasn't given up on you, nor have we."

"Thanks, daddy. Listen, I'm going to let someone else use the phone. I love you all. I'll call again tomorrow."

"Diyah sweetie, do you have to go so soon? Can you call again later today?" Daisy pleaded. She wasn't ready for the call to end.

"Technically, but this is hard, and it's embarrassing. Did y'all hear the news this morning? I made the news. I'd rather cut this call short and call tomorrow," Diyah explained firmly.

"I understand, sweetie. Please remember what I said about keeping the faith," Dawson instructed. "I love you, Diyah. You'll be out of there soon."

"I love you too, daddy. Thank y'all for everything. I know y'all are doing your best," Diyah expressed gratitude.

"I love you, sis. Take care," Danita chimed in.

"Keep your head up, sister in love," Amir offered.

"I love you too, sis. Thanks, Amir."

"Take care, Diyah," Daisy spoke with tremble in her voice. She also wanted to express her love, but feared Diyah wouldn't return it. She'd observed how Diyah responded to her differently from Dawson and Danita.

"Hug Jaylen and Sierra for me, daddy. Bye y'all," Diyah said before she abruptly hung up.

About two and a half hours later, the kitchen was cleaned, the to-go plates were fixed, and the food was put away. And, the Washington Commanders had lost to the Dallas Cowboys. As everyone was about to head to the entryway to grab their coats, Danita changed the living room TV channel to ABC11 since it was 5 PM.

This just in," news anchor Tom George reported, "We've received official reports that there has been another attack on a dark skinned African American father in their mid 70's. The authorities have not released a statement on whether they feel they have apprehended the wrong suspect. Could this be a copycat? The FC Attacker has always attacked at night, but today's attack was during broad daylight. The attack that led to the apprehension of the suspect in custody was also a deviation from the assailant's previous pattern due to the father's race and age. Five questions we must consider: Is the suspect in custody a copycat? Or are they innocent? Or is the person in custody really the FC Attacker? We must also consider whether this attack today was committed by a copycat. Lastly, we must consider the possibility that the FC Attacker is still at large and is escalating. I'm sure local authorities are bearing all these questions in mind, given that the last two attacks are just days apart. So many unanswered questions. No other information has been released at this time by authorities, but they've assured us that this is still an active investigation. Stay tuned to ABC11, and we'll keep you posted as this story unfolds.

Danita mutes the TV and turns around with tears forming in her eyes. Amir rushes to her and holds her. Everyone was looking at one another in shock, each with their own thoughts. *"Is Diyah innocent like she says? Will she be released? Is the FC Attacker still at large? Did she really attack Miguel? What does this all mean?"*

Chapter 11
Attorney Client Privilege

"Jones, you have a visitor," Officer May stated, standing in front of Diyah's cell. Officer May was a 5'3" Caucasian female with black hair and brown eyes. She had a reputation for being unfriendly; however, she did not mistreat any of the inmates. Diyah placed her wrists through the opening of the cell so Officer May could place her in cuffs. Diyah then stepped back, and the cell doors began to open automatically. Diyah walked through to the other side.

"Who is it?" Diyah asked out of interest as the cell doors closed behind her. Diyah did not think that Dawson or Danita would return to visit so quickly. They'd both come to see her on Saturday and Sunday. It was now the Monday after Thanksgiving.

"I don't know, come on. I don't have all day," Officer May instructed, pointing for Diyah to walk ahead of her. Officer May led Diyah to a room. It was a small room with a small metal table and two metal chairs on either side of it.

"Who's this?" Diyah asked Officer May after seeing a woman she did not recognize seated at the table in front of her. Officer May did not answer Diyah. She removed her from her handcuffs and exited the room.

"I'm Constance Shaw," Constance extended her hand to Diyah. She had a firm handshake. Constance had a dark brown complexion & brown eyes that appeared larger through her square gold tortoiseshell eyeglasses. She had gray hair styled in a short coiled pixie cut. She wore a black pant suit with black pumps. "Your sister called me and asked me to take your case. I'm a criminal defense attorney. I promised to come and speak with you before deciding to take your case on. Your sister gave me an update based on the information she had, but I'd love to hear everything from you. So please start from the beginning and leave nothing out. Are we clear, Ms. Jones?"

"Yes, we're clear. Thank you for taking my case on."

"No, Ms. Jones. I haven't agreed to that just yet. I am at the point in my career where I can vet my cases. I own my practice, so depending on what you tell me, and if you're honest, it depends on whether I take your case. I have a reputation to uphold. Now, let's start from the beginning, shall we?" Constance urged. Diyah began to disclose everything to Constance, from last year's Thanksgiving to the most recent event. She noticed Constance taking notes as she talked. Diyah did not omit any details and was honest about her thoughts and actions.

"I see," Constance stated once Diyah was finished speaking. She removed her eyeglasses and sat them down on the table. "Is there anything else I should know?"

"No," Diyah said firmly.

"So to be clear, you're saying you're not the FC Attacker?" Constance clarified.

"No!" Diyah defended. "I haven't attacked anyone! They didn't even ask me for alibis for any of those attacks. My height doesn't even match the eyewitness's description. Did you hear about the attack that happened while I was in here?"

"I must admit the evidence against you is all circumstantial, Ms. Jones. And the attack that occurred while you were in here causes more reasonable doubt," Constance paused to consider everything. She put her eyeglasses back on, "Let's look at the dates of each attack and go over your alibi for each." After 30 more minutes, Constance took a look at Diyah and said, "I can talk to the ADA to see if we can reach some sort of agreement. That is, if you're willing to plead guilty to willful and wanton injury to personal property for the damage to Mr. Sánchez Rivera's office, you will have to be responsible for that."

"Yes, I'm willing to even pay for the damages," Diyah offered. "When do you think I can get out of here?" Diyah asked impatiently.

"If all goes well, it could be as soon as this week or the next. I'll have my private investigator to verify your alibis, and if everything checks out, I'll talk to the ADA," Constance explained.

"Thank you, Ms. Shaw. I'm mighty grateful," Diyah expressed her gratitude. "What's your fee?"

"Don't thank me yet; wait until everything is finalized with the judge. Your sister told me that all your family will come together to cover my hourly rate." Constance paused before switching subjects. "I will say this, Ms. Jones, all of this could have been avoided if you had sought wise counsel and taken heed to it; now, unfortunately, you've had to seek legal counsel instead." Constance reached and took Diyah's hand, "I'm not talking down to you, dear. I just wish things could have gone differently for you. In my career, I've seen too many lives destroyed due to emotional decision-making. Your family loves you, Mr. and Ms. Jones included. All of them are contributing financially, all of them are praying for you, and are concerned about you."

Diyah observed how Constance seemed softer; she'd switch from Constance Shaw, the lawyer, to a concerned Auntie. Diyah just nodded her head as tears formed in her eyes. She was humbled by how her parents had supported her despite her having blocked them out of her life for a year. In that moment, Diyah realized that Dawson was indeed her father, and Daisy needed the same compassion that she was extending to Diyah.

"I'll be in touch. Take care of yourself in the meantime, Ms. Jones," Constance patted Diyah's hand and then began to gather her things. "Guard!"

"Thank you again, Ms. Shaw," Diyah said softly as Officer May entered the room, instructed Diyah to stand, and she placed her back into handcuffs.

Chapter 12
Mercy

It was three days after meeting with Constance Shaw. Diyah had been incarcerated for 8 days, and she was consumed with guilt. She had turned down all visits because she couldn't face her family. She couldn't believe everything she had put them through over the last year, yet they were still showing her unconditional love by pooling their resources and money to cover her lawyer's fees. Their love for her, despite how she had treated them, particularly Dawson and her mom, astonished her. She needed time to build up the nerve to apologize to Dawson and her mom. Fear had disabled her, and guilt made her isolate. She even felt guilty for isolating because she knew she was hurting them again. She felt like she was on a hamster wheel, going nowhere. The one thing she was thankful for was that Amy was in the infirmary for reasons unknown to her, so she had the cell to herself to wallow in her misery.

"What's wrong with you, Jones?" Officer May was standing at the entrance to her cell, suddenly. She didn't even hear her approaching. "I heard you've been turning away your visits."

"I'm surprised you care," Diyah responded with sarcasm.

"What makes you think I do? I'm just doing a wellness check. I don't want any incidents on my watch," Officer May defended. Diyah didn't respond. After a few seconds, Officer May began to walk away.

"Can I see the Chaplain?" Diyah asked.

"I'll make sure you get a DC-572 form," Officer May responded.

"What's that?" Diyah inquired.

"That's the form you'll need to complete to be able to see the Chaplain," Officer May explained.

"Never mind," Diyah sulked.

"Suit yourself," Officer May then walked away.

Diyah wallowed on her bed for a few more minutes, then she heard a voice say, *you know Him for yourself. You have direct access to Him.* She stopped wallowing and froze. This wasn't an audible voice Diyah was hearing; she recognized it as the Holy Spirit. *Will God forgive... me?* She thought to herself. She sat up and rubbed her sweaty palms against the top of her pants. After a few minutes, all her fear and pride fled her body at once. Her head bowed, she lowered herself to the floor in a posture of complete and utter submission. She began to wail, "God, I thank you for your love, and I thank you that you didn't spare your son, Jesus. I thank you for my family and Constance Shaw. I thank you for keeping me safe in here, God. I acknowledged that your son, Jesus, shed His blood for the remission of my sins. I have backslidden. I ask for forgiveness for backsliding, for not forgiving my mom and Dawson, for having pride, and acting out of anger. Come into my heart and cleanse me. I confess that today and moving forward, I will serve you. I ask that you help me forgive Miguel. You know all things God, and you know I am still deeply hurt by his actions. Heal this emotional wound. I rebuke these feelings of shame and guilt because there is therefore now no condemnation to them which are in Christ Jesus, who walk not after the flesh, but after the Spirit. I have been justified by faith, I have peace with you, God through Jesus, my Lord. Thank you for all these things. I count them done in faith. In Jesus name, hallelujah, amen."

Diyah got up from the floor, wiped tears from her eyes, blew her nose, and assessed her emotions. She realized that she did not feel any different, but she had faith and peace that God had answered her prayers and forgiven her. Diyah realized that it was still phone hours, so she headed towards the phones. Surprisingly, there was a phone free. She dialed her mother's number collect and waited for her to accept the charges.

"Hello, Diyah," she heard her mother's voice on the other line. She noticed that her mom's voice cracked, yet she found so much comfort in hearing her voice. "You ok?"

"Hi ma, yes, I'm fine," Diyah reassured her. "It's so good to hear your voice."

"I thank God I'm hearing your voice, too, Diyah. You haven't called me since you've been in there, so I've just stayed away."

"I know, ma. I apologize for not calling you or making you feel welcome to come see me. In fact, I apologize for not forgiving you quickly when you told me I wasn't daddy's child. It hurt, but you apologized, and I should have forgiven you. I've missed a year with you, all of you. Will you forgive me and come see me?" Diyah asked nervously; however, she knew her mother would forgive her and come to see her.

"Oh, yes, Diyah baby, I forgive you. Of course, I'll come see you. I would like nothing more than to come and see you," Daisy whimpered.

"Ma?"

"Yes baby."

"I also want to thank you for contributing towards Constance's fees. I know it isn't cheap. I'm going to get myself together and pay y'all back, but it'll take me some time. I'm sure I've lost my bartending job."

"Diyah, don't worry about that now. You are my daughter, and we are family. We are there for one another in times of need. I hope you truly understand how much we have always loved you, and we will continue to love you."

"Yes, ma'am. I do. I love you, ma, I love all of y'all." By now, Diyah was wiping away tears, trying to control her emotions, considering her environment and the onlookers. "Have y'all heard anything from Constance?"

"No, baby, actually, we were hoping for an update from you. She told Danita she was going to see you on Monday, but Danita hasn't been able to reach her since. We know she's very busy."

"Oh, ok. Well, she did come by on Monday. She agreed to take my case. I don't want to discuss any more details on this recorded line, though."

"I understand, baby. I'm sure Constance will reach out soon because she'll be expecting payment for services rendered."

"I'm sure she will. Listen, ma, I'll see you soon. I also want to call dad to apologize to him. Please give Danita and Amir my love and gratitude for me."

"I will, Diyah. Take care, sweetie. I'll see you soon."

"Thanks, ma, later." Diyah hung up the phone and took a deep breath. She was thankful for how well the phone call with her mother went. She was still nervous because Dawson was next. She dialed his number collect, waited for him to answer, and accept the charges.

"Diyah, what's going on with you? Are you ok? Why did you turn away our visits?" Dawson answered with urgency.

"Hey, daddy, I'm ok. I'm sorry. Constance came and saw me on Monday. Once she shared how y'all were coming together to cover her fees, I felt so ashamed for how I've treated y'all. You and mom in particular. Then I felt guilty for pushing y'all away again. I was a mess. Please forgive me for everything. It hurt not knowing the truth, but you took care of me from day one until now, although I'm not really your daughter."

"Diyah, you are *my* daughter, and *I am your* father. Do you not see it? I only kept some sort of emotional distance throughout the years because I thought you'd reject me once you found out the truth."

"And, that's exactly what I did. Shame on me."

"No baby, no shame. That was a lot for you to process. I wish things could have been different. I apologize for my role in all of this; I could have handled things differently. I'm thankful I have my baby back now."

"Yes, you do. No emotional distance moving forward, promise?"

92

"I promise. And, I ask the same of you, sweetie."

"I promise, daddy. Listen, daddy, I have to go. My time is up. Thank you again for everything. Are Jaylen and Sierra doing ok? Please hug them for me."

"They're doing just fine. I sure will. Take care, Diyah. Remember to say your prayers," Dawson instructed.

"God and I are back aligned, daddy. I most definitely will remember to pray."

"Hallelujah! That's the best news I've heard, Diyah. Proud of you."

"Thanks, daddy. Later." Click. Diyah, unfortunately, didn't hear her father's response because her 15 minutes had run out. She wasn't sad, though. She felt light. She had a bounce in her step as she was walking back to her cell.

"Jones!" Officer May called out.

"Yes," Diyah responded.

"Come with me," Officer May instructed.

"Do I need to be handcuffed?" Diyah asked.

"No, just come with me," Officer May answered. Diyah knew better than to question Officer May further, so she just followed behind her in a state of confusion. Diyah followed Officer May for about 15 minutes. She came to a part of the detention center that she had not seen before.

"Welcome to the R&D department," Officer May said, then walked off after making eye contact with another female guard. Diyah read the words "receiving and discharge". She then looked at the guard and saw her looking in another direction. Diyah followed the guard's gaze, and she saw her lawyer. She was wearing a navy blue pantsuit, nude kitten heels, and a brown wool peacoat.

"Hey, Ms. Jones," Constance greeted her with a warm smile.

"Hey, Ms. Shaw. What's going on?" Diyah asked with curiosity.

"We have a meeting with the ADA and Judge Braswell. You're being released into my custody."

"Wait, what?"

"Yes, ma'am. The ADA and I have reached an agreement. I'll explain everything on the way. These officers are going to process you through the release. I've brought you a change of clothes that Danita provided for you when I met with her over the weekend about you. She had faith that I'd accept your case."

"Oh my God! I'm getting out of here today?" Diyah asked with excitement.

"Yes, you are. Now do everything these officers instruct you so we can get to our meeting," Ms. Shaw chuckled.

"Thank you, Jesus! And, thank you, Ms. Shaw," Diyah expressed with tears in her eyes.

"Thank me after we meet with the judge. Now go on," Ms. Shaw nudged Diyah along.

Two hours later, Diyah had pled guilty to willful and wanton injury to personal property, a class 2 misdemeanor. She had to be on probation for a year, pay for her biological father's damage to his office, and she was instructed to have no further contact with him and to stay away from his home and workplace. Diyah was thankful to be a free woman, but she was heartbroken that she would never get to know her biological father and her paternal half-siblings.

"Shall we surprise your family?" Ms. Shaw asked as she and Diyah were walking out of Judge Braswell's private chambers.

"You mean they don't know that I'm out?" Diyah questioned.

"No, they don't. I can call and ask Danita to get your family together at once so I can meet with them all." Ms. Shaw suggested.

94

"Yes, let's do that. They'll be so surprised. I cannot wait to see them and hug them. Thank you again Ms. Shaw," Diyah opened her arms, hinting for permission to hug her.

"You're welcome, dear," Constance said as she hugged Diyah.

"Now, let's get you to your family, shall we?"

"Yes, ma'am!" Diyah agreed with excitement.

Chapter 13
Home Sweet Home, Finally

It was Thursday, November 30th, and Danita had just gotten off the phone with Constance about 20 minutes ago. She'd called her parents immediately and asked them to come over because Constance would be there in an hour. She felt nervous, but she managed to put on a pair of dark skinny jeans and a burnt orange sweater to look presentable. Constance only said it was imperative for everyone to meet as quickly as possible because she needed to discuss some things with everyone. Danita couldn't help but feel nauseous. She feared the worst. *God, is Diyah really the FC Attacker, and Constance found out*, she thought to herself. Danita tried to shake her thoughts away, but the ache in her stomach told her something was wrong. *Ding. Dong.* Danita jumped.

"It's just the doorbell, sweetheart," Amir soothed Danita by rubbing her forearms. "It's probably your parents, I'm sure they beat Constance here." Danita just shook her head in agreement, then walked towards their front door with Amir on her heels. Amir was wearing a black V-neck T-shirt and brown khaki pants. As Danita approached their door, she saw through the fiberglass that Amir was right, it was her parents.

"Hey, ma. Hey, dad," Danita forced a smile. "Come on in," she greeted each one of them with a hug. Daisy removed her camel double-breasted peacoat. She was wearing a light brown sweater with burnt orange and olive green leaves, a pair of dark jeans, and her dark brown Clarks. Dawson was hanging his lined, dark-brown work jacket at the same time as Daisy. He was wearing a long-sleeved light blue Hanes heavyweight shirt tucked into his relaxed-fit mid-washed carpenter jeans, and a brown pair of composite-toe safety work boots.

"Tell me again what Constance said," Daisy asked. She was feeling on edge.

Diyah began walking towards the living room to lead her family away from the door. "She called and asked me to get everyone together immediately because it was something she needed to discuss with us. I asked for more details, but she said it was best to discuss it together as a family. I pressed, but she didn't budge."

"I hope she gets here soon so we can find out what all of this is about," Daisy expressed as she sat down on the dark and light gray sectional. Dawson sat down too, opposite Daisy, but he remained quiet.

"Can I get something to drink for y'all? Tea? Water?" Danita asked. She was trying to be hospitable, and being busy would help to ease her nerves.

"No, I'm good, Danita, thanks," Daisy responded.

"I'm good too," Dawson responded.

"Well, I think I'll fix me a cup of ginger tea. We still have a few more minutes before Constance arrives," Danita said as she was getting up to head to the kitchen. She felt like she was going to vomit at any time. *Breathe, Danita*, she thought to herself. *Slow breaths.* Danita poured 8 ounces of water into her teapot to warm. Once it had reached a boil, she added a teaspoon of loose-leaf ginger tea to her infuser. She then poured the hot water into her black ceramic mug with the words *Best Teacher Ever* in gold lettering. She placed the tea infuser into the hot water and covered it to steep for 10 minutes. She walked back into the living room and placed her tea on the coffee table so it could continue to steep. She noticed everyone was silent.

"I know we're all anticipating what Constance has to say, but did y'all want to watch TV in the meantime?" Amir asked as Danita was getting comfortable beside him.

"No, I wouldn't be able to focus," Daisy responded.

"I'm good, son," Dawson responded with a nod.

Danita just smiled at Amir. He already knew she was too keyed up to watch TV. Twenty more minutes went by, and Danita had finished her ginger tea. It had been approaching an hour since Constance's call. She was secretly hoping that Constance would arrive earlier than communicated. *Ding. Dong. Ding. Dong.* "That must be Constance. Thank God, she's a little early," Danita expressed as she arose to walk to the front door. Her legs felt like jelly. She noticed that it seemed to be two people outside the door. It was hard to see through the fiberglass because of daylight savings, and it was near 5 PM. "It looks like it's someone with Constance if it's her," she called out to the living room. Amir arose and began to follow in Danita's direction. Danita turned on the porch light and flood lights. To her surprise, she saw that it was Constance and Diyah. "Diyah's with Constance!" she called out as she was opening the door. "Oh my God!" Danita said, embracing Diyah.

"Hey sis," Diyah said as she greeted Danita with a hug and smile. Diyah was wearing a black peacoat over a pecan-brown silk long-sleeve blouse tucked into a knee-length black pencil skirt, and black stiletto pumps.

"I can't believe you're here! You look so good," Danita complimented.

"Diyah!" Daisy called out, running towards Diyah. She pulled her into her arms. Diyah and Daisy began to weep with joy.

"Hey, Constance," Danita said, finally acknowledging her. She had tears in her eyes. "I'm sorry. Come on in and hang your coat. How in the world did this happen?"

"No apologies needed," Constance chuckled. "This is what I wanted to discuss with y'all," she said with a wide grin, pointing towards Diyah. "I'll explain after everyone gets settled, and I won't stay long, so I'll keep my coat on."

Dawson was hugging Diyah now, and she continued to sob. After everyone had greeted one another and settled down, Constance updated everyone on the terms of Diyah's release. "Thank you, Constance. We're truly grateful," Danita spoke first.

"Yes, we all are," Dawson chimed in.

Daisy was continuing to hold Diyah in her arms. She was rocking them back and forth. "I could never repay you for taking on Diyah's case. Her release means the world to me," Daisy expressed, choking back tears.

"Well, you might not or can't pay me the world, but my office will send over the invoice tomorrow," Constance stated with a smile. Everyone laughed.

"We'll make sure that's taken care of," Dawson stated firmly.

"I have no doubt," Constance responded. "Listen, I'll leave you all to have some time to yourselves," Constance said, getting up to head to the door.

"I'll walk you to the door," Danita offered.

"Before you go, Constance, did they ever find and arrest the FC Attacker?" Dawson asked.

"No, not to my knowledge, they haven't. That person is still at large," Constance paused briefly to answer. After Constance left, Danita ordered an assortment of pizza, which was Diyah's favorite, and they paired it with a tossed salad. The family ate, laughed, and cried some more as they reconnected.

"I just want to thank everyone again for all you've done for me." Diyah expressed herself after wiping her mouth and hands clean of chocolate chip pizza. "From the support, the visits, the understanding, the money for Constance, these clothes, taking care of Jaylen and Sierra. I love you all."

"We love you too, dear," Daisy answered for everyone.

"I also just want everyone to know that I rededicated my life back to Christ right before I called you mom and dad," Diyah informed everyone, but she was looking at her parents. "I was on my knees praying for strength because I had some apologies to extend, and I felt so ashamed. I also decided that I first needed to get back in right standing with Him before asking Him for strength."

"Hallelujah! Praise God!" Dawson exclaimed.

"Thank you, Jesus! Daisy and Danita said in unison. Daisy, who was still sitting right next to Diyah, reached over and hugged her. "That's the best news," Daisy expressed. "I didn't think it could get any better than you being home, but it just did." Daisy wiped the tears from her face.

"I'm so happy to hear this, sis," Amir said, and he got up to hug Diyah along with Dawson and Danita.

Danita immediately thought back to earlier in the year, when Amir and she hosted their Christmas redo on January 6th. She remembered that when her father was praying specifically for Diyah, the Holy Spirit showed her Diyah kneeling and praying. The Lord reassured her on January 6th that Diyah would return, and now she had. "We should all go to church together on Sunday," Danita suggested. "Is everyone ok with coming to Victory Life with Amir and I?" She asked.

"I'll be there," Diyah was the first to answer.

"Sounds good to me," Dawson responded.

"Of course I'll be there," Daisy responded. "This will be the first time we've all worshiped together in decades," Daisy reflected. Since Dawson and she divorced about a year after Diyah was born, it was just she and the girls who worshiped together, except when Dawson came for special occasions, such as when the girls were in a Christmas play or singing a solo.

"Great! We'll see you all on Sunday at 10 o'clock, but get there about 9:45 so we can all sit together," Danita said excitedly.

"Sounds good, sis." Diyah agreed. "Dad?" She called out to Dawson.

"Yes, sweetie," he responded.

"I'd like to get Sierra and Jaylen and go home if you don't mind," she asked. "I'm anxious to see them."

"So soon?" Daisy asked.

"It's near 8, ma," Diyah laughed. She then considered Daisy's feelings a little more deeply. "Did you want to spend the night at my place? My bed's big enough, but it'll be a tight fit. I just have a full-sized bed."

"That would be lovely, dear," Daisy brightened. "I'll go home and pack an overnight bag, and by the time Dawson drops you off with Jaylen and Sierra, I should be there. Everyone hugged each other tightly and bid each other a good night. Danita felt amazing. She noticed that this was the best she'd felt emotionally since miscarrying.

"How are you feeling?" Amir asked. Danita found him in the kitchen after collecting her teacup from the living room. He was beginning to clean up from dinner.

"Grateful. I feel good," Danita responded.

"You did all that worrying for nothing," Amir teased.

"I know, right?" Danita chuckled. "God had everything all worked out. How are you feeling, for real?" Danita shifted and asked, searching Amir's eyes.

"I'm grateful too. I'm rejoicing right along with y'all," Amir responded. He'd pulled Danita into his arms. He smiled down at her and admired her. Their eyes locked, and silent communication passed between them, building an unspoken invitation. An invisible force pulled them together in a kiss.

It was after 11 PM, and Diyah had just gotten out of the shower. She'd oiled her damp body with argan oil, a few drops of lavender essential oil, and shea butter. She found the earthy aroma of the argan oil, the shea butter, and the floral scent of lavender soothing. She dressed in her gray pajamas, which had *Please Do Not Disturb* written in white letters. She was feeling thankful to be in her own space, to shower in solitude, and to have her fur babies back with her. Diyah yawned; exhaustion was weighing heavily on her. After she arrived home, she played with Jaylen and Sierra while she and her mom talked some more, but now sleep felt inviting her in. She'd dropped her thermostat down to 65. Diyah climbed into her bed. Jaylen and Sierra, who had been following Diyah's every move, jumped onto the bed too. They settled in between Diyah and Daisy, who was sound asleep. Diyah knew that her fur babies would enjoy their body heat, but they were also being territorial. Jaylen and Sierra were secretly communicating that she was their human. They were her border, and Daisy couldn't get too close. Diyah turned over to face the wall so Jaylen and Sierra could warm her backside. She struggled to pull her white flat sheet and pink bedspread up to her neck because Jaylen and Sierra were weighing down the covers. She whispered a prayer to God, expressing her gratitude for being in her own bed right before she fell asleep.

Thump. Thump. Thump. "Diyah Jones! Knightdale Police Department! We have a warrant for your arrest!" A voice called out to her in her dream. Boom! Her front door was busted open. Detective Mills yelled again once inside her home, "Diyah Jones! Knightdale Police Department! We have a warrant for your arrest!" He said again, coming into her bedroom. "You thought you got away with it, didn't you?" Detective Mills said, pointing at her with a scorned look on his face.

Diyah sat straight up in her bed. She was drenched in sweat, shaking, and her heart was racing. She held her breath, looked around, and strained her ears. She noticed that her mother was still sound asleep, and so were Jaylen and Sierra. Nothing, not even her, had disturbed them. *You're ok, Diyah, it was just a trauma nightmare*, she thought to herself. She looked at the clock. It was 2:07 AM. Diyah realized that despite her physical freedom, it would take some time and effort to emotionally heal from everything she had endured. Since she was on high alert, she decided to go into the living room and spend time praying, seeking God for spiritual messages and rebuking any demonic attacks.

Chapter 14
Capture a Moment

It was Saturday evening, December 16th. Diyah had been released for a little over 2 weeks. She had been door dashing, pulling 8-9 hour days, to help make ends meet because she chose not to return to her bartending job since she'd re-dedicated her life to Christ. She didn't want to be in that environment anymore. She'd also been looking for jobs. She figured that with her recent charges, she would not be hired as a traveling RN providing direct care, so she was looking into research and nurse auditor job opportunities. She'd called some colleagues from her past to ask for their assistance, and she had also prayed about it. God knew what she needed, and with the help of former colleagues, she was hopeful.

Diyah just walked into her apartment from a 9-hour day door dashing. Jaylen and Sierra greeted her by meowing and rubbing up against her ankles. Diyah was wearing a pair of black, high-waisted, sleek tech joggers, a gray Winston-Salem State University Alumni hoodie with red lettering and the Ram mascot centered underneath, and her white Core/Black Gum Adidas originals. "Hey Jaylen, hey Sierra," she greeted them. "Y'all missed mommy," she asked. An hour and a half later, Diyah had given her fur babies some attention, showered, and changed into her red-and-white plaid pajamas. She was getting ready to sit down on her couch and eat a garden salad when her phone rang. "Hey, sis," she greeted Danita as she sat down.

"Hey, Diyah. Whatcha doing?" Danita asked.

"Just about to eat dinner. I'm having a salad tonight with tuna," Diyah responded.

"Doesn't that sound healthy?" Danita commented.

"And, it's light. I don't want to go to bed with something heavy on my stomach," Diyah explained. "Anyways, how've you been?"

"I've been good, actually, really good. My therapist informed me that grief isn't linear, though, so I'm thankful for this moment of goodness. I know grief is a journey."

"You're in therapy?"

"Yes, chile. The grief, plus your situation, I couldn't connect with one fast enough online after you were locked up. I'm in a better place today, though."

"I'm happy to hear that. I love that for you. I need to follow up on therapy myself. I need to process everything that's happened. How's Amir?"

"There's nothing wrong with having Jesus and a therapist, sis, but yeah, Amir's been really good too."

"I've been meaning to ask, what made him cut his hair?"

"He wanted a change after the miscarriage. He said it felt like it was too much for him to manage."

"Oh, I see. Well, I understand that. We as women will cut our hair for any reason, so I definitely get his decision. It looks good on him."

"It does, doesn't it?"

"Oh, Lord. You're being conceited," Diyah and Danita shared a laugh. "Now, I have some questions about mom and dad. I know I've been missing in action, but when did they get so close?"

"Basically, after Thanksgiving last year, when your secret and my secret came out of the closet. They knew how much both of us needed them, and to be effective, they needed to work together."

"OOOOH, I see. But they seem mighty close, don't you agree?"

"They are close, but I think you're hinting at something more, Diyah." Danita and Diyah shared another laugh. "I think they are friends again. I don't think it's anything more, but it's something to get used to. I've had a year to adjust to it."

"Yeah, I've only had 2 weeks. It's good to see, though, but weird. A good weird, I guess."

"Yeah, it's definitely good, and it was weird at first."

"Listen, I have an idea. What do you think of us taking pictures? We've never had a family portrait because of mom and dad's divorce. It seems they are in a place where this could be possible." Diyah sat her empty bowl down on her end table. She'd just finished eating her salad.

"I love that idea, Diyah. I'm confident mom and dad would go along with it. We can do a Christmas theme and wear matching pajamas."

"Thanks for the suggestion, sis, but I have a vision. Ironically, it's a Christmas theme like you suggested. There's a photographer I know who is running a last-minute Christmas special. The setup will be at a tree farm, and we'll take the pictures there. I would like for mom and dad to wear cream, you and Amir to wear either forest green or hunter green, and I'll wear red. We'll all wear yellow gold accessories."

"But you would be the only one in red?"

"Yes, that's on purpose. I'm embracing my difference instead of feeling self-conscious about it. Besides, mom has made it plain that my name means love in Lembaama, although It is spelt differently, so I should be the one wearing the color of love."

"I love it. These will be some beautiful portraits, Diyah. I can't wait to see the final edits."

"We have to take the pictures first. Are you and Amir available to do it on Wednesday, the 20th?"

"Diyah, that doesn't give me enough time to adequately shop!"

"I know, I know. But otherwise, we'll have to change the theme and do it after Christmas. Pleeeeease. This will be my gift to y'all."

"Ok, if mom and dad can do it, I'll make sure Amir and I are there. Call them, and if it's a green light, then schedule it, and send out the details."

"You're so bossy, but thanks."

"I am the big sister. I'm entitled. And you're welcome." Danita and Diyah chuckled.

"Ok, well, let me go so I can call mom and dad, and hopefully get this scheduled tonight."

"Ok, good night, Diyah."

"Good night."

———————————

Four days later, the Jones and the Franklins were at Noel Tree Farm, located in the rural part of Red Oak, NC. As requested, everyone was dressed according to Diyah's instructions. Dawson was dressed in a cream sweater, khaki pants with creases, brown leather shoes, and a traditional classic gold watch on his left wrist. Daisy was wearing a cream sweater dress that fell to the top of her knee, paired with a wide, dark brown accent belt, dark brown leggings, and a pair of dark brown leather highline ankle boots with a block heel. She chose gold infinity earrings to adorn her fresh twist-out and wore red lipstick.

Danita was wearing a round-neck, forest-green, high-waist pencil sweater dress with bat-winged sleeves. She opted to have bare legs greased with cocoa butter/vanilla oil and wore nude stiletto pumps, red lipstick, a layered paper clip and cable gold chain, and matching paper clip hooped earrings. She had her big, boxed braids pulled up into a high bun. Amir was wearing a forest green sweater with navy blue anchors all over, blue khaki pants, toffee-brown leather low-top sneakers, a Movado bold gold watch on his left wrist, and a Cuban curb gold chain necklace.

Lastly, Diyah was wearing a red ribbed turtleneck sweater dress, gold hoop earrings, and nude stiletto heels. She achieved her curl pattern by wetting her hair, applying leave-in conditioner, defining her curls, using gel, scrunching up her hair to lock in the pattern, and then using a diffuser to dry her hair. She also finished her look with red lipstick. "Everyone looks so good. I appreciate y'all for doing this," Diyah expressed.

"You look so good, too. I love your hair," Danita said as she was touching Diyah's curls.

"Thanks," Diyah blushed.

"This was a great idea, Diyah," Daisy complimented. " Thank you for organizing and paying for this. I can't wait to hang pictures on the wall in my living room."

"I hadn't thought of that, but I think I'll hang some pictures too because my walls are bare," Diyah considered. "Isn't this farm magical?" Diyah looked around at the seemingly never-ending rows of green trees. They would be taking pictures underneath the gold string lights where the green trees in that section were adorned with gold lights. She inhaled the invigorating scent of pine, fir, and cedar trees. She smiled and walked over to put her arm around Dawson's waist to give him a one-sided hug. He hugged her and kissed her on her forehead.

"You look lovely, Diyah," he expressed. "Thank you for including me," he whispered in her ear.

"Family photos wouldn't be complete without you, daddy. You chose me, and I choose you." Diyah teared up as she whispered back in response. She briefly thought about Miguel, and she felt a lump trying to rise in her throat; however, she quickly distracted herself. She was determined to be present and enjoy this historical moment with her family. She looked up and saw a woman approaching them.

"Hey, Diyah girl, y'all look so good. Are y'all ready to take some photos?" Her name was Tameka, and she was the photographer Diyah knew. She was an African American woman who stood

5'5", with a medium brown complexion, and she had a small frame. She appeared to be in her late 30s and had braces. She had her dark brown hair pulled up into an afro puff. She was wearing a red sweater, dark denim jeans, and brown duck boots.

"Hey girl, thanks. Yes, we are. Let me introduce you to everyone. After making introductions, Tameka took group shots with various props. She took some pictures of Dawson, Daisy, Danita, and Diyah: Dawson with his girls, Daisy with her girls, and the sisters took some pictures together. Danita and Amir took some couple pictures, including one of them kissing underneath the mistletoe. The family laughed and really enjoyed showing off for the camera, as if they were high-paid models. These were memories Diyah never wanted to forget. Despite the fact that she didn't have a career, she was experiencing financial strain, she was on probation, her biological father didn't want to have anything to do with her; she viewed her life as imperfectly perfect. She was blessed in spite of it and was thankful for the idea of having a photographer to capture these moments for her and her family.

Chapter 15
The Run Away

"Last night was amazing," Danita said, looking at Amir. They were cuddling in the living room on their sectional, wearing their respective King and Queen matching black T-shirts with plaid red and black flannel pants. She was reflecting on the photoshoot her family had had the previous day. Her family had never formally taken family photos, and the joy and laughter when they were all together were new for them.

"Which part?" Amir asked.

"Huh?" Danita was puzzled.

"You said last night was amazing, which part?"

"Stop it," Danita blushed. "I was referring to the photoshoot," she laughed.

"Oh, yeah. That was nice." Amir commented dryly.

"Don't be like that. Amazing doesn't even describe what we shared," she commented, running her fingers through his beard.

"Oh, really?" He asked, pulling her closer.

"Yes, really," Danita blushed some more.

"That's what I wanted to hear." *Ding. Dong.* "Are you expecting someone?"

"No, "I'm not expecting anyone."

Amir got up from the couch and headed towards their front door. He saw through the fiberglass that it was a Caucasian woman, with black hair pulled up into a bun, who appeared to be in her 50s. She wore a black pant suit with a white button-up. He chose not to open the door, but talked through it instead. "Can I help you?" He asked.

"Yes, I'm hoping to speak with Amir Franklin. I'm Investigator Nancy Anderson from the Nash County Sheriff's office," she showed her badge. "Are you Mr. Franklin?"

Amir opened the door, and the smell of cigarette smoke greeted him. He noted that Investigator Anderson must be a cigarette smoker. "Yes, I'm Amir. What's this all about?"

"May I come in?" Investigator Anderson asked as she extended her hand to shake Amir's.

"Hi, I'm Danita," She stepped in front of Amir and reached for Investigator Anderson's hand. Amir had no idea when Danita got up from the sectional. "I'm Amir's wife. What did you need to speak with my husband about?" Danita deliberately distracted the Investigator from her request to enter their home.

"I wanted to speak to your husband, Mrs. Franklin," Investigator Anderson said, looking at Amir, even though she was talking to Danita and shaking her hand.

"Whatever you need to speak with me about, you can share in front of my wife. We don't keep any secrets," Amir stated firmly.

"Ok, Mr. Franklin. I'm here on behalf of the Person County Sheriff Department. It's about the child you gave up for adoption 16 years ago. They've gone missing."

"M-m-my child? What happened?" Amir felt like the blood was draining from his head, leaving a hollow, weightless feeling. He leans up against the door frame to support himself. Danita reached out to support him, too; she put her arms around him.

"Tell us everything," Danita pleaded.

"Have you been in contact with your child, Mr. Franklin?" Investigator Anderson asked.

"What? No, I don't even know what my child looks like. I don't know if I had a boy or a girl," Amir explained firmly.

Investigator Anderson looked at Amir for a few seconds. She was studying him. "From my understanding, his adoptive parents told him about his adoption shortly after his 16th birthday. He expressed wanting to meet his biological parents; however, his parents felt like it would be best for him to wait, so he wouldn't get distracted from his academic track. From what they've shared, he wouldn't let it go. He kept asking to meet y'all. They believe he ran away with plans to find his birth parents. His friends reluctantly confirmed the adoptive parents' theory. When he left home, he had plans to travel here to find you and his biological mom."

"He. You said he. So I have a son?" Amir asked.

"Yes, Mr. Franklin, you do. Have you seen any teenagers hanging around your neighborhood that weren't familiar to you?"

Amir was frozen. "No, Investigator Anderson, we haven't seen any teenagers in our neighborhood that we didn't recognize," Danita answered.

"Mr. Franklin, what about you?" Investigator Anderson pressed.

"No, I haven't," Amir said, shaking his head.

"Do you still keep in contact with his mom?" Investigator Anderson inquired.

"Kara? I haven't spoken to her in almost 16 years. It hurt too much to stay together after the adoption. After graduation, I rarely saw her."

"The Sheriff Department there has had some trouble tracking her down," Investigator Anderson explained.

"I can't help you. I'm sure her family would know. They live in Tarboro," Amir offered.

"Edgecombe County Sheriff's Department spoke with her family. Her parents are deceased. From their reports, she sold the house and never came back after her father died a few months ago."

"This is news to me. I'm sorry I can't be of more help," Amir expressed. "What's all being done to find my son? How long has he been missing?" He asked.

"He's been missing for two days now," Investigator Anderson reported.

"Two days! It doesn't take two days to get here from anywhere in Person County," Amir exclaimed.

"Person County is doing everything within its power to find your son, Mr. Franklin, including reaching out to other departments for assistance. That's why I'm here. Here's my card. If you happen to hear from your son or Kara, please call me right away."

Amir took Investigator Anderson's card. "Wait! Shouldn't you show me a picture so I can be on the lookout for my son? And what's his name? Does he have a car?"

"Yes, we both can be on the lookout," Danita offered.

Investigator Anderson studied Amir for a few more seconds. She reached inside her inner blazer and pulled out a wallet-sized picture. "His parents wanted you to have that. I was waiting to see if you'd ask for a picture. I just had to make sure you didn't know what he looked like. His name is John. John Jacobson." Investigator Anderson extended the photo to Amir. "Everyone calls him JJ. Yes, he has a car, but he was smart enough not to take it. His cell was left at home, too. We could have tracked him by GPS otherwise."

"Thank you," Amir took the photo. He tried to steady his hand, but it was shaking. He held his breath as he looked at the photo. He saw his face, a younger version of himself, but a yellowish-brown version. Amir noticed that John wore his hair in two-strand twists on top, with a fade on the sides and back. Amir felt a wave of emotions. After all of these years, wondering about the child he placed in adoption care, what they looked like, if they were a boy or a girl? Now he knew. This seemed surreal. He tried to hold himself together, but he couldn't any longer. "Please find my son, Investigator Anderson," he said as he began to cry. "I'd love to meet him."

"We're doing everything in our power. You have my card, please be in touch." Investigator Anderson nodded towards Danita as she turned and walked away towards her unmarked black Ford Taurus.

"Come inside, sweetheart," Danita coaxed. She led Amir back towards their living room. "They're going to find him. I'm sure he's ok." Danita sat down, hoping Amir would follow her lead. He began to pace.

"I can't believe this is happening. I only found out that my child is a boy because he's missing. I don't want to lose him. I never even got to know him."

"You won't lose him, Amir. Maybe he went to find Kara first. You know how children are over their moms, especially boys," Danita tried to rationalize to soothe Amir's worries.

"The police can't even find her," Amir expressed with frustration.

"They will, and they'll find John, too," Danita encouraged.

"I can't believe this," Amir wiped away his tears and began looking at the picture of his son again.

"Can I see?" Danita asked. Amir sat down and showed her the picture. He wasn't ready to let it go. Danita began to rub Amir's back. "Handsome boy. He looks just like you. He must have his mother's complexion, though."

"Thanks. Yeah, he does." Amir took a deep breath. "I need to call my parents. They need to know, as they might have some information about Kara's whereabouts. You know my mom keeps up with the gossip."

"Yeah, you should definitely call them. Isaiah, too." Danita remained seated on the couch as Amir began to call his parents. She began praying silently for John's safety and for peace for everyone who loved him.

Chapter 16
Christmas Eve

It was Danita's 33rd birthday as well as Christmas Eve. She and Amir were getting ready for Sunday service. Service would be an hour, considering the Holiday, and they were encouraged to dress down. Danita was wearing a red and white plaid button-up tucked into dark denim skinny crop jeans. She pulled a cream sweater over her red and white plaid button-up and folded the collar of the button-up over the sweater. She'd gotten her hair silk pressed for her birthday. She put on a pair of pearl stud earrings, unwrapped her hair, applied red lipstick, and put on her incensed wedge platform suede chucks. She sprayed Jo Malone Pomegranate Noir on her clothes and wrists.

"You smell as good as you look, birthday girl," Amir commented. He was just walking back into their bedroom from warming up the car. He was wearing a long-sleeved red sweater with brown elbow patches. The top of the sweater had white bucks and white Christmas trees. He was also wearing dark denim relaxed-fit jeans, his Movado bold gold watch on his left wrist, his Cuban curb gold chain necklace, and his brown toffee leather low-top sneakers.

"Thanks, bae. You look good, too," Danita complimented. She noticed that Amir was trying to be in good spirits, considering it was her birthday, but she knew he was worried about John. He'd been moping for days prior. They still had not heard anything since the Investigator visited their home three days ago. Amir had made it clear that he did not think the police would be doing much during Christmas, which made him worry even more about John's safety.

"You ready?" He asked.

"Yes, let's go."

Twenty-five minutes later, they'd arrived at Victory Life, and they were walking into the Sanctuary. They planned to sit on the main floor as usual. They hugged and greeted members as they were walking to their seats. Some people knew it was Danita's birthday, and those people also wished her a happy birthday. They walked to the front and sat in the middle section. Danita waved to Constance and her father, Deacon Goodbody, who was sitting in the right section in the same row as them. Just then, Danita felt a tap on her shoulder. She looked to her left and saw Diyah and her parents.

"Happy birthday, sis," Diyah said, reaching to hug Danita.

"Oh my God, y'all surprised me," Danita expressed with excitement. She hugged everyone, as did Amir, and Danita's family wished her a happy birthday.

Service began promptly at 10 AM. The praise team took it back in time and began the service by partying to 'Jesus is the Reason for the Season' by Kirk Franklin and the Family. To create an atmosphere of worship, the praise team then sang 'O Come Let Us Adore Him' by Maverick City Music. Many members of the congregation began to worship loudly, some crying and even kneeling at the altar as the praise team repeatedly sang "for you alone are worthy" and "you deserve the glory". Considering it was a condensed service, only those two songs were sung, followed by the welcome, and then the word.

Pastor Frank was the executive pastor of Victory Life. He was 51 years old and led a congregation of about 2,000 multigenerational members. Pastor Frank was 6'5", had a bald head, caramel complexion, and slim build. He was wearing a brown blazer, a red button-up, dark denim jeans, and brown leather dress shoes. "Good morning, Victory Life! Merry Christmas Eve," he greeted the congregation. "Jesus is the reason for the season, amen."

"Amen," the congregation responded.

"I know we've already had the welcome, but I'd like to personally welcome all visitors to Victory Life this morning. We're glad to have you worshipping with us. In fact, I'd like to thank you all for coming out. I know it's Christmas Eve, and this is one of the busiest times of the year, but you made time for God. He honors those who honor Him, amen."

"Amen," the congregation said in unison.

"If you have your Bibles, turn with me to **Luke Chapter 1**. If you don't have your Bibles, follow along on the screen. I'll be reading from the NIV version, and for the sake of time, we will start with **verse 26** and end with **verse 33**. And it reads,

In the sixth month of Elizabeth's pregnancy, God sent the angel Gabriel to Nazareth, a town in Galilee, to a virgin pledged to be married to a man named Joseph, a descendent of David. The virgin's name was Mary. The angel went to her and said, "Greetings, you who are highly favored! The Lord is with you." Mary was greatly troubled at his words and wondered what kind of greeting this might be. But the angel said to her, "Do not be afraid Mary; you have found favor with God. You will conceive and give birth to a son, and you are to call him Jesus. He will be great and will be called the Son of the Most High. The Lord God will give him the throne of his father David, and he will reign over Jacob's descendants forever; his kingdom will never end."

"Keep your place In Luke, but now let's turn to **Matthew Chapter 1:18-19**," Pastor Frank instructed. Danita observed how Amir had shifted in his seat. He had removed his arm from around her. She was sure he was thinking about their miscarriage, and John, since the passage highlighted how Mary would give birth to a son. Truthfully, she momentarily thought about their miscarriage, too. *Was it a boy or a girl,* she thought to herself. "And it reads,

This is how the birth of Jesus the Messiah came about: His mother, Mary, was pledged to be married to Joseph, but before they came together, she was found to be pregnant through the Holy Spirit. Because Joseph, her husband, was faithful to the law, and yet did not want to expose her to public disgrace, he had in mind to divorce her quietly."

"Now, don't raise your hand, but how many of you men in here would have been like Joseph, ready to divorce?"

Some members of the congregation smirked.

"The passage says that Joseph didn't want to expose Mary to a public disgrace, but I'm sure he didn't want to expose himself to a public disgrace either. Men, you know how prideful we are?"

"Amen," a few members of the congregation yelled.

"Fellas, did you hear the women saying amen? They know how prideful we can be."

The congregation chuckled.

"All right, let's look at verses 20-24,

But after he had considered this, an angel of the Lord appeared to him in a dream and said, "Joseph son of David, do not be afraid to take Mary home as your wife, because what is conceived in her is from the Holy Spirit. She will give birth to a son, and you are to give him the name Jesus, because he will save his people from their sins." All this took place to fulfill what the Lord had said through the prophet: "The virgin will conceive and give birth to a son, and they will call him Immanuel (which means "God with us"). When Joseph woke up, he did what the angel of the Lord had commanded him and took Mary home as his wife."

"I'd like to pause here and highlight how Joseph could have chosen to have been in his feelings despite what the Angel of the Lord told him. But it's better to be in God's will than our feelings. Church, do you want to be in your own will, in your feelings? Or do you want to be in God's perfect will?" Pastor Frank became quiet; however, he received no response from the congregation. "Some of y'all will catch that next week.

Now, let's turn back to **Luke, chapter 2, verses 1-5.**

In those days Caesar Augustus issued a decree that a census should be taken of the entire Roman world. (This was the first census that took place while Quirinius was governor of Syria). And everyone went to their own town to register. So Joseph also went up from the town of Nazareth in Galilee to Judea, to Bethlehem the town of David, because he belonged to the house and line of David. He went there to register with Mary, who was pledged to be married to him and was expecting a child."

Pastor Frank paused again and looked at the audience before he continued speaking, "Now, church, Joseph is a better man than most, or Luke decided to omit Joseph's feelings in this account.

First, he discovers that his wife to be is pregnant. He didn't do like many of us. He didn't go off. He didn't accuse her or even call her names. He just planned to back out of their arrangement quietly. Joseph was like, "I didn't sign up for this! How the young folks say it, "dis tew much."

The congregation howled.

"Then once the angel of the Lord came to him in a dream, he was ready to obey what the angel of the Lord told him to do, regardless of any ridicule he might've encountered. You know how people are always offering their unsolicited advice and opinions. Then a decree comes from Caesar for a census. Now Joseph and his very pregnant fiancée had to travel to Bethlehem. Check this out, looking at the passage of scripture, we don't see Joseph complain. We don't even see Mary complaining. Ladies, you know how y'all are in your ninth month of pregnancy. I remember how my wife was. Look at her over there laughing. Y'all be ready to fight if we ask you to walk a mile. Can I get an amen?"

"Amen," both men and women responded, while others laughed. Danita offered a small smile, but she refused to look to her left or right, not wanting to make eye contact with anyone.

"Many Biblical scholars estimate that it took Joseph and Mary roughly a week to travel to Bethlehem. There's no specific mention in the text that they had any mode of transportation. Some assume that they had a donkey to assist with travel because of the culture, but it's not specified here in **Luke 2**. I don't know how comfortable Mary would have been riding a donkey at that advanced stage of pregnancy, especially for long periods, whether they had a donkey or not. Here's what we do know: there were no cars, trains, or airplanes, so traveling during this time for Mary would have been rough, and it would have been rough on Joseph, too. Joseph would have had to consider the safest route for him and Mary. Their journey would have had to be slower to accommodate Mary's stage of pregnancy. If they didn't have a donkey, he would have had to carry the majority of whatever necessary items they had with them. At times, he might've had to support Mary in their walk. She might've needed to lean on him at times. Just imagine it, imagine them having to climb hills and rocky terrain. I don't know if they ever felt like giving up or turning back, but this journey from

Nazareth to Bethlehem was not easy. Today, in church, we can be encouraged by Joseph and Mary. I purposely waited to disclose, but the topic for this morning's sermon is *"The Lord is with you."* Isn't that what Gabriel told Mary? Saints, we can find numerous accounts in the Bible of people overcoming obstacles and doing mighty, supernatural things because the Lord was with them. Earlier, I said that Joseph was either a better man than most or Luke failed to include Joseph's emotions. I'd like to believe that Joseph had the peace of God, which surpassed all understanding. Once he heard from the angel of the Lord, that peace guarded his heart and mind. The peace was a shield against the devil's thoughts, against the chatter of small-minded people, and against other emotions he might have experienced. You see, church, Mary wasn't called for this purpose alone; Joseph was too. Oftentimes, when we're walking toward our God-given purpose, we can experience ridicule, uncertainty, and fear along the way. We may experience hills and rocky terrain metaphorically. At times, our journey can become extremely uncomfortable, just as Joseph and Mary's did. How many of you can relate?"

Almost all the Sanctuary raised their hands.

"This time of the year is a celebration church; however, some people could be feeling low, down, anxious, and depressed because of where they are in their journeys. Everyone's journey isn't ordained by God because he gives us free will, but He's still there. He won't leave us nor forsake us. I know many of you might want to know how to get out of the journey, but I'm here to say the journey is a part of the process. You have to go through it. I know people don't want to go through things. They want to be delivered from it, but how does that test the faith and build perseverance, church? God sends tests to pinpoint where we are spiritually, to purify us. I know y'all don't want to say it, but can I get an amen?"

"Amen," some of the congregation responded.

"Amen," Pastor Frank said again.

"Amen," the congregation said in unison.

"We must know that if God is allowing us to experience challenges while we're walking in our God ordained purpose, those challenges are necessary to fulfill His purpose. Specifically in Joseph and

Mary's case, He allowed their rugged journey to fulfill the prophecy of the birth of a Savior that would save his people from their sins. Now, if you're NOT walking in your God-ordained purpose, doing things your way, like you're at Burger King, and experiencing challenges, that's God's way of getting your attention. He left the ninety-nine for the one, but that's another sermon. Praise team, come on up. I'm getting ready to close. Church, I want to reiterate to you again that the Lord is with you. Be encouraged by that fact. Trust in Him with all your heart and lean not on your own understanding; in all your ways acknowledge him, and he will make your paths straight. Find some scriptures to encourage you on your journey. One of my favorite scriptures is in **Lamentations 3:22-23**, because of the Lord's great love we are not consumed, for his compassions never fail, they are new every morning; great is his faithfulness." Pastor Frank paused as the keyboard player began to play softly in the background. "You know, saints, I'm reminded of Paul while he was imprisoned awaiting trial. I encourage y'all to study the Book of Philippians. It's just 4 chapters. Paul was in jail yet was thankful, content, encouraged the Church of Philippi, promoted unity, and remained at peace despite his circumstances. If you read Philippians, you'll see that Paul understood that being in prison was for the advancement of the Kingdom. He didn't cry, complain, or express how unfair it was for him to be locked up for doing the will of the Lord. He didn't pray and ask to be delivered. He didn't ask 'why me'. Instead, he kept his focus on the will of the Lord, just as Joseph and Mary did. Church, **Philippians 1:29** from the Message Bible states:

"There's far more to this life than trusting in Christ. There's also suffering for him. And the suffering is as much a gift as the trusting."

"We trust God for the good, such as the healing, the financial breakthroughs, the job, the marriage union, the healthy baby, which are all blessings and gifts from God; however, suffering for Christ is as much of a gift as the latter. Remember, the Lord is with you on this Christmas Eve. He'll be with you for the number of your days; all you have to do is access him. Be thankful, He is using you to advance His Kingdom, don't ask, 'why me'. Joseph and Mary never questioned why them on their journey. I encourage you, church, to have the heart posture of 'Why not me'. God will complete His work in you, you will carry it to completion until the day of Christ Jesus, so rejoice!!!! Please stand on your feet and worship with the praise team. The altar is open for anyone who wants to gain access to Him by repenting and accepting Him as their savior. It's also open for those who have been complaining about their storms, and for anyone who needs someone to stand with them and agree for strength and perseverance. Lastly, just come to the altar if you want to worship the birth of Jesus Christ, our Lord. Sing praise team, prayer team, and elders come on down."

The praise team began to sing, "Why Not Me" by Tasha Page-Lockart. Amir took Danita's hand and led them to the altar. They both had questioned why the miscarriage had happened, and Amir was currently questioning John's disappearance. Danita was crying, as she witnessed with the elders as they prayed over her and Amir. She heard the praise team singing:

And I'm asking myself questions like: Why did I do it? Why did this happen to me? Then I said, You can get through it, you just have to believe. What I do now, gotta make it all count.

So why not me? I'm the perfect person to go through the storm It won't break me, it won't kill me, I'll move on And then I'll come out even better than before. And I'll never see this place anymore 'Cause my faith is gettin' stronger every day I'm removin' everything that's in my way And the fact that I survived another day Makes me say, why not me?

As Danita and Amir were returning to their seats, she glanced through her tears and saw that Diyah was at the altar herself, receiving prayer. Danita raised her hand to thank God for how God was using her, Amir, and Diyah for the Kingdom.

Chapter 17
Christmas

Christmas morning. Diyah had just framed all the pictures she was planning to gift. To her parents, they each were getting 11x13 family pictures of just them and she and Danita. To Danita, she was gifting a 5x7 picture of herself and Danita, and a 5x7 of Danita and Amir kissing underneath the mistletoe. She would provide her family with a link to order additional pictures at their leisure. Diyah put red bows on the front of the glass in the frames and slid all the framed pictures into a Joy to the World gift bag for transport later.

She looked around her apartment. No Christmas decorations were in sight. She foolishly threw away all her decorations out of hurt when she had to purge to downsize. At the time, she was done with the Holidays because it reminded her of family, the family that had betrayed her. Now, she regretted that decision because she could not afford to buy decorations, considering she had very little money left over after covering her bills, groceries, gas expenses, Danita's birthday, and Christmas.

She opened up her Shein package. Diyah had also purchased frames to hang pictures for herself. She decided to order black frames because she had brown carpet and beige walls, and she needed something to break up the natural tones. She framed an 11x13 of her family to include Amir, and an 11x13 family picture of just the Jones. She'd also framed a 5x7 of Dawson, she and Danita; a 5x7 of Daisy, she and Danita, and a 5x7 of just herself and Danita. Diyah then took out her tape measure and command strips to prepare to hang her pictures, along with her 10.63"H x 20.56" x 0.75'D Family Matters black wood-framed sign, on the wall in her hallway leading towards her bathroom and bedroom. After playing with different designs on the floor, Diyah decided to hang her Family Matters black-wood-framed sign at the top, her three 5x7 pictures directly underneath the Family Matters sign to create the allusion of a T, and then she surrounded the allusion of the T with her two 11x13s. One at the bottom of the T allusion on the left, and the other 11x13 at the top on the right.

Once she finished, she wished she had Christmas photos of she, Jaylen, and Sierra. *Next year*, she thought to herself. Diyah took a step back to admire her family wall. Diyah notices how she stands out like a sore thumb; everyone is tall and has a darker complexion, even Amir. Normally, this would have made her feel awkward, especially now that she knew the truth; however, this time, she just acknowledged her difference and reminded herself that she is loved and accepted. She brought the warmth to every picture in her red sweater dress. She smiled at herself and her family. She looked at her phone, another *Merry Christmas* text was coming through, and she realized a little over an hour had passed. She needed to get ready so she could arrive at Danita and Amir's home in time enough to prepare and bake the macaroni and cheese.

A little over an hour later, Diyah was pulling up to her sister's and brother-in-law's. She was wearing red skinny jeans, a black sweater with a decorated green Christmas tree on the front, a white cat climbing the tree wearing a Santa Claus hat, and her pair of black UGG boots. She gathered her Joy to the World bag, which held everyone's gifts, along with the items for making the baked macaroni and cheese, and walked up to their front door to ring the bell. She admired the green wreath on the front door, adorned with clear lights, pine cones, cherry berry clusters, and a large red bow.

"Hey sis, Merry Christmas!" Amir greeted her. He took her grocery bags and hugged her. He was wearing a red and black plaid button-up, black relaxed-fit jeans, and black ankle socks.

"Merry Christmas!" Diyah responded, hugging Amir back. "I'll hang on to this bag," she said, referring to the Joy to the World gift bag, "but you can put those bags in the kitchen."

Amir forced another smile, "Ok, sounds good." Truthfully, he didn't even see that Diyah had another bag in her hand. He was distracted thinking about John. The investigators still had no updates.

Diyah walked to the living room to place her gift bag behind the tree, ensuring no one could easily look inside before it was time to exchange gifts. She admired the tree. It was a green artificial tree with clear lights, adorned with red and gold ornaments, ribbons, and a gold star at the top of the tree. She turned to meet Danita's gaze as she was approaching her. She was wearing a plaid green, red, and brown belted arc-hem dress and gray bedroom shoes. Diyah observed that Danita's silk press was still holding its body. "Merry Christmas, sis," Diyah said as she opened her arms for a hug.

"Merry Christmas, Diyah," Danita said, and hugged Diyah back. "Are you just admiring our tree, or did you sneak something underneath it?"

"Both."

"Diyah, you've done enough," Danita scolded. "You all ready went in on the 90-minute massage gift certificate for my birthday with mom and dad. Please save your money."

"It's Christmas, Danita. Let's have peace," Diyah distracted her. She began walking towards the kitchen to start preparing the baked macaroni and cheese. First, Diyah put on a pot of water so it could reach a boil. She added her noodles and salt to taste. Once the noodles were done, she drained them and added them to a mixing bowl. She added 2 packs of shredded sharp cheddar, one pack of shredded Velveeta, and one pack of shredded mozzarella. In a separate bowl, she added 2 cans of evaporated milk, 3 eggs, salt, pepper, a smidge of garlic powder, and mixed them together. She added her mixture to the noodles and cheese. Once everything was combined, she put the contents of her bowl into her aluminium baking dish, topped it with shredded mild sharp cheddar and butter balls. She had the oven preheated at 375 and set the timer for 45 minutes.

Thirty minutes later, Amir began to drop battered trout into hot grease out back. And shortly after that, the doorbell began to ring. It was Daisy. She was wearing a red blouse, dark denim jeans, and her brown Clarks. "Hey, ma, Merry Christmas," Danita greeted her with a hug. "Your twist out is still looking great."

"Merry Christmas, sweetie, thank you. I saw Diyah's truck outside. She's here already, huh?"

"Yes, she's in the kitchen. Amir just started dropping the fish."

"Oh, ok, your father pulled up right behind me."

"I see him. Go on and put your gifts underneath the tree," Danita encouraged. She turned around and saw Dawson approaching the door. She opened it before he had a chance to ring the bell. "Merry Christmas, daddy," she said, hugging him.

"Merry Christmas, Danita." Dawson was wearing a red, long-sleeved button-up that was tucked into his creased khaki chino pants and brown leather shoes. He was carrying his famous scratch red velvet cake in a cake box.

"Ma's probably with Diyah in the kitchen, Amir is outside, he just dropped the trout," Danita informed him.

"Thanks, baby girl, I'll stop by the kitchen and drop this cake off. Here," he handed her a Christmas card enclosed in a red envelope. "This is for you and Amir."

"Thanks, daddy, I'll put it underneath the tree because I'm sure it's something inside," Danita smiled.

"It's my pleasure," he said, kissing Danita on the forehead.

Danita walked outside to check on Amir. The smell of frying goodness greeted her. "Hey, you, are you going to stay outside? It's chilly out here." She walked over and wrapped her arms around him. She knew he was trying to be in the Holiday spirit.

Amir rubbed her back. "I'm enjoying the crisp air. Besides, as hot as this grease is, it won't take these trout long to get done, and then I'll drop the second batch. Are my parents and Isaiah here yet?"

"No, not yet, but I'm sure it'll be any minute now. You need anything?"

"No, I'm good, thanks, sweetheart."

"Ok, well, I'm going to go back inside because it's chilly to me."

"I'll be back inside in a minute; this first batch is almost ready."

Danita walked back inside her home through the kitchen. She noticed that the baked macaroni and cheese was done, and Diyah had taken it out of the oven. "Your baked macaroni and cheese looks good, Diyah."

"Thanks, it's gonna taste just as good as it looks, too."

Danita laughed. *Ding. Dong.* "I'm sure that's the rest of our crew, I'll be back," she said, leaving her mom and Diyah in the kitchen. Her dad had made himself comfortable in the living room, watching TV. She paused on the way to the door. She couldn't help but overhear Diyah express to their mom that she wished Miguel would drop the restraining order and be open to getting to know her. Danita felt Diyah's pain. *Ding. Dong.* The doorbell pulled her back to the present. She continued walking towards the front door, and she noticed it was just Ma Belle and Pop William. "Merry Christmas!" She greeted them.

"Merry Christmas!" They responded in unison. Ma Belle walked through the door first. She was wearing a grey *"Jesus is the Reason for the Season"* sweater with mid-wash denim jeans, her brown ankle Clarks, and her locs were down. Pop William was behind her, and he was wearing a red *"Christmas Begins with Christ"* sweater with white Christmas trees and snowflakes on the sleeves, paired with black chino pants and dark brown flat-heeled Chelsea boots.

"Where's Isaiah, and.... what's her name again?" Danita asked.

"He said they would be here in about ten minutes, and her name is Dené," Belle responded.

"Y'all still haven't met her?" Danita asked with curiosity.

"No, and I'm anxious to meet her," Belle responded.

"I'm looking forward to meeting this young lady, too," William interjected. "In the meantime, where's everyone else?"

"I last saw Amir outside. The first batch of fish is probably done. My dad's in the living room watching TV, and my mom and Diyah are in the kitchen," Danita responded.

"How's Amir doing?" Belle inquired.

"He's trying to be in better spirits, considering the Holiday. Yesterday's sermon seemed to help, too. He's still struggling, though, I can tell. How are y'all doing?" Danita explained and inquired.

"I'll head outside," William excused himself.

"Truthfully, we'd never thought this would happen. Our grandson is missing, and it seems the investigators are suspicious of his birth parents. All of this is crazy. Where is our grandson? Why aren't there any updates?" Belle paused and shifted. "We're going to remain hopeful. That's all we can do, right?" Belle expressed.

Danita nodded silently in response to Ma Belle. Then, she and Ma Belle walked towards the kitchen. Ma Belle spoke to Dawson as she passed by the living room. Amir had just finished putting the first batch of trout in the oven to keep warm. He hugged his parents afterwards. "Merry Christmas, pops! Merry Christmas, ma!"

Merry Christmas they responded in unison. "I'll head out with you, son, to drop the second batch of trout," William offered.

"Ok, pops, where's Isaiah and Dené?"

"They should be here shortly," William responded.

"We should be ready to eat around the time they arrive, then," Amir announced to everyone. He and William headed outside.

Ding. Dong.

"That must be Isaiah and Dené," Danita said. "Did you want to get the door, Ma Belle?"

"No, you go on. I wanna play it cool," she responded, shooing Danita away.

Danita walked to the front door and confirmed it was Isaiah and Dené by looking through the fiberglass. "Merry Christmas! Welcome Dené, I'm Danita. Isaiah's sister in law," she hugged

Dené. Danita observed Dené, who looked to be in her early 30s. She was eye level with Danita, so she must've been around 5'6" or 5'7", unless her shoes gave her an extra inch or two. She had a medium-brown complexion and wore her hair in comb twists about 3 inches long. She was wearing a white *"I'm His Only"* gingerbread T-shirt, brown gingerbread earrings, mid-wash skinny jeans, and a tan pair of Journee Mirette stacked heel boots.

"Merry Christmas," Dené responded, stepping into the entryway. She began removing her coat.

"Do I get a Merry Christmas and a hug?" Isaiah teased. He was 35 years old, stood 6'5", had a peanut brown complexion, slim build, and his locs were styled in 7 thick flat twists that flowed into a low, loose ponytail. He was wearing a white *"I'm Her One"* gingerbread T-shirt, relaxed-fit mid-washed jeans, and a pair of red suede Puma Astro Play sneakers.

"Of course, Merry Christmas, Isaiah," Danita hugged him. "I just wanted to greet Dené first. Cute T-shirts, you two."

"Thanks," they said in unison. Isaiah took Dené's hand.

"The food is done, so y'all are right on time. Everyone is in the kitchen," Danita guided Isaiah and his guest towards the kitchen.

Ten minutes later, everyone had been introduced, and Amir was filling a paper-lined basket with the fried trout for serving and placing the remainder in the oven to keep warm. Their non-traditional Christmas menu consisted of fried trout, coleslaw, hushpuppies, baked macaroni and cheese, stewed white potatoes with onions, string beans, and red velvet cake. Everyone sat down at the 8-seater table, which was decorated with traditional Christmas foliage as the runner and two red candles in gold candle holders. They were dining with simple gold and white dinnerware. Amir was sitting at the head of the table, and Danita was sitting opposite him at the other end of the table. William, Belle, and Isaiah were sitting to Amir's right. Dawson, Diyah, and Daisy were sitting on Amir's left, with Diyah being in the middle. Amir pulled out a folded chair from the garage for Dené to sit beside Isaiah on the end. Amir said the blessing, and everyone began to fix their respective plates.

"So Dené, tell us about yourself. Isaiah has told us so little," Belle inquired.

"Really? I feel like I know y'all. He talks about y'all all the time," Dené said, looking at Isaiah in confusion.

"It's not like that, babe, you know how important you are to me. My family can get to know you for themselves," Isaiah reassured Dené.

Dené studied Isaiah for a few seconds, trying to read him. "What would you like to know, Mrs. Franklin?" She asked.

"What are you passionate about? What makes you smile? I mean, aside from my son here," Belle asked.

"Wow, those are good questions. Hmmm. I'd say my faith, family, and social causes are my passions. Equally, my faith and family make me smile, and seeing how forward change positively impacts the community also makes me smile."

"That's impressive," Belle commented. "So what do you do for work?"

"I work for an advocacy firm in Raleigh. My firm provides a noteworthy percentage of housing counseling in the country. We believe that housing counseling is the most effective way for marginalized people to become homeowners. We have an impressive track record of successfully assisting people with becoming home buyers. Seeing someone make their wildest dream come true, and actually becoming a homeowner, makes me smile," Dené elaborated.

"Oh wow. Amir, honey, maybe you can utilize Dené as a resource. You come across people who want to buy a home, but have little to no knowledge on how to become a homeowner," Danita offered as she was adding some hot sauce to the trout on her plate.

"Yeah, that's actually a good idea, sweetheart," Amir agreed.

"So, Dené dear, you also mentioned your faith. What are your beliefs?" Belle continued to inquire.

"Jesus died and rose three days later, so I could live life abundantly," Dené stated firmly.

"Amen, Jesus is the reason for the season," Belle pointed to her sweatshirt with a smile. She was genuinely impressed with Dené so far. She gave Isaiah an approving smile.

The Franklin and Jones family continued to enjoy their Christmas lunch, engaging in small talk as they got to know Dené, and she them. After everyone had seconds and dessert, they all pitched in to help clean. There were little to no leftovers. The families engaged in a Christmas exchange, and to Dené's surprise, Danita had a gift for her, too.

"We didn't want you to feel left out," Danita explained.

"Oh, I would have been fine. You didn't have to, but thanks so much," Dené expressed. She opened her small, gold gift bag, which enclosed a $15 Target gift card, a travel-sized body butter, and a balsam & cedar candle. "Oh wow, thank you again, Danita. This was thoughtful of you."

"You are a guest in our home, so," Danita laughed.

Diyah was the last to present gifts. She gifted her parents and Danita with their framed pictures. "I texted y'all the link too, so you can order the exact pictures you want," she explained.

"Oh, Diyah darling, this is perfect," Daisy teared up. "Give me a hug."

"I agree," Dawson choked up. He and Daisy were both looking at their respective pictures after he and Daisy finished hugging Diyah. Dawson also proudly showed the pictures to William and Belle. He was a proud papa.

"I agree too, sis, thanks," Danita chimed in. "I can't be mad that you spent money on these gifts." She acknowledged.

"You printed my favorite pic. Thanks, sis, " Amir smiled. He was referring to the picture of him and Danita kissing underneath the mistletoe.

"No thanks needed, I appreciate y'all more than you know," Diyah responded.

The Franklin and Jones family continued to socialize. They played Christmas, Who Am I, Christmas Bingo, and took turns in pairs playing Blindfold Bow Scoop. Danita noticed that Amir seemed most like his normal self when competing against his brother. He even demanded a tie-breaker round to settle the score, in which Amir won. She secretly believed that Isaiah allowed Amir to win, considering all things. Two hours later, everyone said their thank-yous and hugged each other goodbye before leaving.

"Finally, I can get out of this bra and Spanx," Danita expressed after everyone had left. "That was fun though, right? Dené seems like a good catch. You think she's the one for Isaiah?" She was heading towards their bedroom.

Amir followed. He was going to get comfortable, too. "Yeah, it was fun. Isaiah has never brought anyone to Christmas before, so I do think she could be the one. Besides, you see those couple T-shirts they had on?" Amir laughed. "*I'm her one*," he mocked Isaiah's shirt.

"I diiiiid," Danita laughed. "Leave your brother alone."

"I'm happy for him, for real. He chose well."

"He followed in his little brother's footsteps," Danita smiled and did a twirl. She is referring to the fact that Amir chose well.

"Facts," Amir matched Danita's smile.

"Hey, did you want to watch *It's a Wonderful Life*?" She was secretly hoping that Amir wouldn't break their tradition, but she was prepared in case he wasn't in the mood.

"It's tradition, of course," he reassured her. "I'm allowing the peace of Christ to guard my heart and mind. The Lord is with John as He is with me. Romans 8:28." Danita was thankful for the gift of Amir. Despite the stressor of John's disappearance, Amir still honored and celebrated her 33rd birthday on Christmas

Eve, allowing the spirit of Christmas to bring him some joy and hope, too.

"Amen," Danita stated firmly in agreement. "God has a purpose in this. He will use this. So we can place our confidence in Him."

"Yup," Amir agreed.

"You see, George, you really have a wonderful life? Don't you see what a mistake it would be to throw it away?" Danita paraphrased a famous line from *It's a Wonderful Life*.

"I won't mistakenly throw it away," Amir responded firmly. "I understand this is necessary, this test won't be just for my benefit, but for others too."

Chapter 18
It's a Small World

It was the day after Christmas, and Diyah was preparing for Rah's visit. She was wearing a pair of army green cargo lightweight joggers and a burgundy crop shirt. She had not seen Rah since the night she confronted Miguel. She and Rah had spoken briefly once by phone since she'd gotten out, but this would be her first face-to-face. Rah reminded her of the night that changed her life, but she did not want to keep blowing her off. First, she cleaned out Jaylen and Sierra's litter boxes. She exposed the cats' waste outside in the apartment's dumpster. Then, she ran the vacuum from the living room, down the hallway, and into her bedroom. She also used her handheld vacuum to vacuum her couch. Lastly, she dusted her end table and spot-cleaned her bathroom's sink and toilet. Just as she was washing her hands, she heard a knock on the door. *She's here*, Diyah thought to herself. Diyah dried her hands on her hand towel and proceeded to her front door. After checking the peephole, she let Rah in.

"Hey, Rah, come on in," she greeted her with a hug.

"Hey, jailbird," Rah teased. Diyah gave Rah a stern look. "What, too soon?" She asked.

"Yes, it's too soon for the jokes," Diyah stated firmly. "I don't know if I can ever joke about that."

Rah walked into the living room, sat down on the couch, crossing her legs. She was wearing a khaki hoodie with matching sweatpants and white Sketcher sneakers. "I'm surprised you agreed to my visit. I know you've been avoiding me," Rah confronted Diyah.

"You're right, I have," Diyah sat down on the other end of the couch.

"Why? Are you embarrassed?"

139

"Obviously, yeah, but that's not the only reason. The night I confronted my biological father was the last time I saw you. He accused me of attacking him. His accusation, plus them finding those clothes in my home, is what led to my arrest. The last time I saw you was the last time I saw Miguel. You are a reminder of a night that brings me pain because that's the night Miguel acted like he did not have an older child. The night he rejected me," Diyah explained.

"Wait, so he acted like he didn't have a child with your mom?"

"Exactly, but when I said her name, recognition spread across his face. He was so cold," Diyah recalled.

"That's messed up."

"Yeah, tell me about it. What's even more messed up is that he was attacked later that night, and he named me as his attacker. Now he's taken out a restraining order and everything. I'll never get to know him or my siblings," Diyah teared up.

"I'm sorry, D," Rah reached over and rubbed the top of Diyah's hand. "Is it too painful to talk about?"

"It's painful, but I need to talk about it."

"Ok, so why did he think you were the one who attacked him?"

"I kinda went off when he kept denying me."

"What did you do?"

"I got loud, cornered him, threw some things. I scared him."

"Oh, shoot, served him right."

"Nah. I felt so bad about it almost immediately. He was wrong, but I handled it poorly. I went back the next morning to apologize and offer to pay for the damage, but the gym was closed. I didn't know then, but he'd been assaulted by the FC Attacker." Rah gave Diyah a suspicious look. "What?" Diyah asked.

"You can tell me, girl. Are you the FC Attacker? Or did you follow through and pretend to be, so you could attack your good-for-nothing daddy?"

"NO!" Diyah stated firmly. "I have never attacked anyone in my life."

"Ok, girl, your secret is safe with me."

"Rah, I'm serious," Diyah began to laugh. "I'm innocent."

Rah laughed too. "Whatever you say. I don't want no smoke. So what was it like being locked up?"

"It was horrible. We take things for granted: privacy, fresh air, freedom to choose. I was scared the entire time I was in there. Scared I might be assaulted, and scared I would be found guilty of being the FC Attacker. I can't believe they still haven't found him."

"What makes you think he is a he, and not a she?"

"Huh?"

"I'm just saying, girl power," Rah laughed.

"You are crazy, Rah. There's no way the FC Attacker is a woman."

"Could be. The FC attacker is smart. They haven't gotten caught, and they've been laying low since you were released. Anyways, do you think the cops are still watching you?"

"I don't know. If they are, they're wasting their time."

"Mmm-hmm."

"Rah, stop it," Diyah laughed again. "I'm not the FC Attacker for the last time. Anyways, there's a bright side to this story. I was able to truly forgive my mom and Dawson. I recognize that Dawson is my daddy, just like you said, Rah. I felt guilty for losing a year with them. They came to my rescue, my sister too. I thank God for all of them."

"See? I'm happy for you, D. You got your family back and your freedom."

"Yes, and I rededicated my life back to God, too. That's why I didn't try to get my job back at the bar."

"You ain't the first to find jailhouse religion," Rah commented.

"This is for real, Rah," Diyah expressed. "I didn't rededicate my life as a manipulative tactic to be released. I did it because I needed His strength to apologize. I did it once I recognized how much my family loves me, and I remembered that He loves me even more than they do. I did it because He's worthy and I want to honor Him for the rest of my life."

"Ok, I hear you. So I guess no more partying for us then huh?"

"Nope. No partying, but you can go with me to church one Sunday. I don't have a church home, but I have been enjoying my sister's church. It's Vic-"

"I'm good on that, thanks though," Rah cut her off. "So how's things been for you since returning home? What are you doing for money?"

"I'm door dashing 8-9 hours a day. That's why I asked you to come over this evening and not earlier. I'm looking for jobs in the meantime, too. I plan to use my degree and knowledge as a nurse in some way."

"Who's gonna hire you with a record?"

"I trust somebody will. God knows what I need. Besides, I'm not applying for direct care jobs. I'm looking into research or auditing. I have been considering becoming an independent contractor and teaching CPR, First Aid, etc., to various organizations to meet an unmet need for continuing education and new hires."

"Sounds like you have it figured out."

"I wouldn't say that, but I'm hopeful. My family has been supportive too."

"That's good. So tell me about them. You have never talked about them until the last time I was over here."

"My parents are retired, and they're divorced for obvious reasons. They are good friends now, which is weird. According to my sister, her name is Danita, their friendship rekindled after Thanksgiving last year. It's weird, but it's nice. We were able to take Christmas family photos. We've never taken family photos. I'll show you before you leave."

"That is nice. My family used to take family photos yearly. My mom insisted."

"Oh yeah? Are you close to your family? You have never talked about them either."

"And, I won't start today," Rah said, changing the subject, "So is your sister older? Younger? Do you have any brothers?"

"No, brother, just me and my sister. She's four years older. And she's married. Unfortunately, they had a miscarriage back in the early part of November. That forced me out of my isolation towards her so I could support her and my brother-in-law."

"Oh no, I'm sorry to hear that. I know that must've been hard on them." Rah teared up.

"Yeah, it was. Are you ok?"

"Yeah, I was just feeling for your sister, that's all, losing a child is a mother's worst nightmare."

"Thanks. They seem to be getting better, or at least they were."

"They had a setback?"

"You can say that. My brother-in-law had a child before he and my sister got together, and he just learned that the child is missing."

"Oh my God! How long has the child been missing?"

"A week as of today, from my understanding."

"Oh my, what are the police doing?"

"They say it's still an ongoing investigation. We don't know how seriously they're investigating, considering he's 16 and left home on his own. They haven't even found his birth mom."

"I'm confused."

"His parents disclosed to him that he was adopted. He had an interest in meeting his birth parents, but his adoptive parents discouraged it, at least for the time being. They wanted him to remain focused on his academics."

"Why did they tell him during the school year then?"

"Your guess is as good as mine. It took me some time to even find out my brother-in-law had a child because he disclosed this to my sister after I learned that Dawson wasn't my biological daddy, and I was avoiding her, too, when she found this out." Diyah paused. "Dang, we sound like a lifetime movie, don't we?" Diyah tried to make light of the situation.

"All families have secrets and drama. I'm convinced that's a fact." Rah shifted, "Hey, I'm curious, why did your brother-in-law place the child for adoption. That's not common."

"You know, I've never asked. He was young, though. So maybe that's why."

"Yeah, I understand that 100%. I hope they find his kid."

"Thanks, I appreciate that, Rah. We're all petitioning the Lord. Asking for his safety and return."

"I agree with that. I hope the kid is safe. Why haven't they found the birth mom?"

"I don't know. My brother-in-law fell out of contact with her. They were kids when the child was conceived. No one seems to know where she is, if she's even alive."

"What's really going on?"

"That's what we want to know, too." Diyah shifted. "So, what's going on with you and everyone else at the bar?"

"Same old, same old. Different day, same story. I'm just working and partying. Living the life," Rah smiled. "You're gonna get bored, watch."

"I wasn't bored before with my old life. I wasn't partying then, I think I'll be all right," Diyah stated confidently.

"All right, we'll see."

"We shall."

"Working at the bar and partying is all that we had in common, so what now?" Rah asked.

"We'll probably fall apart. Sounds harsh, but it's true. We have nothing keeping us connected," Diyah stated.

"Very true. Well, you have my number and I have yours. I'm truly happy for you, Diyah. Things worked out for you, and I know they will continue to do so."

"Thanks, Rah. I truly appreciate that. Thanks for being an ear when I needed it. You are a good listener when you're sober and serious."

"I told you, there's a lot you don't know about me, girl. I'm full of surprises. Anyways, let me go. I just wanted to lay eyes on you. I must admit, I was hoping we'd have a welcome home party."

"I had a quiet welcome home celebration with my family. That was perfect. But it was good seeing you, though, Rah, despite the reminder you know."

"Yeah, I know. Anyways, walk me to the door."

"Wait, I want you to see my family first. I did a family wall in the hallway," Diyah motioned for Rah to follow her as she got up from the couch. Rah got up and followed Diyah towards her hallway. Diyah stopped to turn on the hallway's light. "Here's my family,"

145

Diyah presented her wall. The first picture was the 11x13 of just the Jones', Diyah pointed everyone out to Rah, she showed the 5x7s, and finally the 11x13 to include Amir. "And, here we are again, with my brother-in-law, Amir."

"Who?" Rah took a closer look.

"My sister's husband, Amir," Diyah repeated.

"Is that Amir Franklin?" Rah couldn't stop staring at the picture.

"Yeees, do you know him?" Diyah asked. Rah was frozen. She was recalling everything Diyah had just shared with her about her family. "Rah," Diyah said, shaking her. "What's going on? How do you know my brother-in-law?"

"I need to see him. Can you take me there?"

"Excuse me? Why would I take you to see my sister's husband?"

"It's not like that, Diyah! God! You said that the police haven't been able to find the birth mom, right? I have information on her. Can you please take me to see him?" Diyah stared at Rah for a few seconds. "Diyah, I'm not joking, nor do I have ill intentions. Please reach out to him?" Rah begged.

"Ok, let me call my sister and him. I'm going to excuse myself to the bedroom to call."

"Go on," Rah urged her with desperation.

Five minutes later, Diyah returned from the bedroom and found Rah still in the hallway looking at the photo that included Amir. Diyah was now wearing a black solid pair of Adidas. "I have my sister on the phone. Amir isn't home, but my sister said to come on. Amir will be home by the time we arrive. Should the Investigator also meet us there?" She asked.

"Yes, I need to talk to them too. Come on, hurry up," Rah headed towards the front door. "I'll meet you downstairs. I'm going to follow you."

"Ok," Diyah responded, but Rah didn't wait to hear her response. Twenty minutes later, Diyah was pulling up to Amir and Danita's home with Rah on the tail.

When they arrived, the floodlights came on, and Amir came outside to greet them before they reached the door. "Diyah, what's going on?" He asked, walking towards Diyah. Danita was on his heels.

Diyah turned to point to Rah to explain, "This is Rah. We used to work together at the bar. I told her what was going on, and when she saw your picture, she said she had information on your son's mother."

"It's a boy?" Rah asked. Just then, she and Amir's eyes met.

"Kara?" He asked with uncertainty. "Is that you?"

"Hey Amir, it's me. We had a little boy?" She whispered.

"Wait, Rah isn't your real name?" Diyah asked, confused.

"Let's go inside and get this all sorted out. It's cold out here, and Investigator Anderson is waiting for us on the inside," Danita encouraged everyone to go inside.

———————————

Amir wasn't the only one who didn't know he was going to have an unexpected encounter with someone from his past, and although Daisy was unaware of what was going on with her daughters and son-in-law in Nashville, she knew what was about to happen at her location. Daisy had just pulled up to a gray building with glass doors and glass windows covering the entire front of the building near its closing time. The building was easy to find with its name written in bright red letters. She put her car in park, but left it on so the heat would keep her warm. She was going to wait outside until she saw him, Miguel. She planned to confront him. She called the gym earlier and asked to speak to him, and hung up when she heard his voice. She didn't want to talk to him over the phone; she just needed to confirm he was at the gym.

Fifteen minutes went by, and she saw staff leaving the building. Within minutes, there were only two cars left in the parking lot. Hers, and his. In another seven minutes, she saw the building go dark and someone exiting from the front door. It was him. She hadn't seen him in nearly three decades, and it was dark, but she recognized him. Daisy cut off her car and exited. She quickly walked up towards him. "Miguel!" She called out.

He jumped. He was startled. "Who's there?" he asked. "I don't want no trouble."

"Miguel, it's me, Daisy. I'm not going to hurt you. I just want to talk," she said, finally standing in front of him. They were standing underneath a light pole. Daisy was sure he was parked there for safety, considering his attack last month.

"Daisy?" He asked, confused.

"Daisy Jones. Diyah Jones' mother. You know, Diyah, right, our child," she looked at him without blinking. "You denied her too many times, and the last time was about a month ago, but you can't deny me, Miguel. Daisy was wearing antique-colored jeans, a dusty rose sweatshirt, and her camel-colored peacoat. She had her hands in her pockets. Her right hand was gripping folded-up pieces of paper.

Miguel was wearing a black toboggan, a black active workout fit windbreaker with Sánchez Rivera Gym embroidered in red lettering in the upper left corner, black joggers, and a pair of red and black Adidas. "Daisy," he said with a sigh of relief. "I guess I shouldn't be surprised to see you. What are you doing here?" He asked with a hint of irritation in his voice.

"I'm here to let you know our daughter didn't attack you. Dawson and I didn't raise her to be violent."

"Oh yeah, well, did you raise her to be destructive?" He asked sarcastically.

"No, but can you blame her? She reveals herself as your daughter, and you deny her straight in her face. She was deeply hurt. I don't condone her actions, but I understand them. She knew that you denied her despite the paternity results, and then you denied her 29 years later. Imagine how that made her feel?"

"Imagine how I felt being attacked, not knowing if I was going to live, and then to wake up in the hospital."

"I'm sorry you were attacked, Miguel, but that wasn't Diyah. That was the FC Attacker."

"I believe that it was Diyah. The police didn't do their job to prove it was her; that's all. She was arrested for a reason."

"That was a misunderstanding. Those charges were dropped."

"Insufficient evidence, if you ask me. Your girl is guilty."

"Miguel, I'm not going to go back and forth with you. Again, I'm truly sorry you were attacked. But that wasn't Diyah-"

"Why are you here, Daisy?"

"I would like for you to drop the restraining order and pay for the damages Diyah caused."

"Are you crazy? Why would I do either?"

"Hear me out?" Daisy put up her hand, indicating for Miguel to stop. "You owe her, Miguel. She's your daughter. Your own flesh and blood. Would you want someone treating Marisol the way you're treating Diyah?"

"How do you know my daughter's name?"

"I did some research," Daisy said, her head held high. "You know what else I know? I know where you live, your wife's name-"

"Are you threatening me and my family?" He cut her off.

"Of course not! But I'm not above a lil blackmail."

"Diyah was conceived before I even started dating my wife. You can't blackmail me," Miguel snickered.

149

"Remember how I used to email you every so often, begging you to be a part of our child's life? Remember how you responded, making excuses, making empty promises?"

"Yeah, so."

"I kept all of our emails. Even the ones where you offered to meet me at the hotel, so we could talk and work something out. Room 219. Do you remember that? You didn't know that I knew you had gotten married, but I did. The dates are in the emails, Miguel. I'm sure your wife would be interested in knowing her husband was trying to bed his former lover. Thank God I didn't fall for your boyish charm again."

"You wouldn't. I thought you were a Christian now."

"I am. And I know blackmail isn't Godly. But aren't you a practicing Catholic?"

"Sí."

"Well, God isn't pleased with either of us right about now." Daisy softened before she continued. "Diyah just wants to get to know you, Miguel, and she wants you to get to know her. She wants to get to know her siblings, too. Please consider dropping the restraining order. She is between jobs right now, so having her restitution debt erased would help her a lot."

"And if I don't, you're going to show my wife those emails, huh?"

Daisy took a deep breath, and the cold air hit the back of her throat. "No, I won't. You have my word. I came here with ungodly intentions, but you reminded me that I am a woman who represents God and tries her best to obey Him. Forgive me. I just hope you do the right thing, because you, too, are a man who represents God. I'll pray His word is a lamp unto your feet. You take care, Miguel." Daisy turned to leave without waiting to hear his response. She committed that this would be the last time she would appeal to him to do right by their child. A lump formed in her throat, and she began to tear up as she quickly walked back to her silver Buick LaCrosse. She felt like she'd failed Diyah all over again. A good mother was supposed to ensure the well-being of their child, and her act of selfishness over 29 years ago created a void in Diyah, a void she could not fill. Tears began to flow parallel down Daisy's cheeks and met underneath her chin like two rivers merging into one channel.

Daisy reached her car, turned on the ignition, and sat still. She needed to calm her nerves before she drove away. She noticed that Miguel did not immediately drive off. That surprised her. She took out some napkins from her car's glove box. She always kept extra napkins from fast food restaurants, just in case. She wiped her eyes, blew her nose, and used hand sanitizer. Then she said a quick prayer, "Lord, I come to you in the precious name of Jesus. I ask for your forgiveness for attempting to coerce Miguel. I ask that you flow from my spirit to my soul, spreading your peace, not just for me, but for Diyah too. I pray her heart is filled with your love and joy. I pray she always knows her true value in you. I pray for Miguel. Forgive him, Lord. I pray for a revival in his heart. Create in him a pure heart, oh God. I pray that he forgives himself once he realizes what he's done, and that your love and peace consume him. Let your will be done. And help me remember that your will may not look like my desire, but I trust that your will is always good and best. Thank you in advance. I count it done, in faith, in Jesus' name. Amen." Daisy took a deep breath and drove off. She never looked back in her rearview mirror because she wanted to leave the past behind her, but everything within her knew that Miguel was still parked in the gym's parking lot when she left.

Chapter 19
Case Closed

It was Wednesday, December 27th and Danita was sitting on the couch in her living room, watching *The View*. She had on a pair of blue silk pajamas that she put on after her shower. *The View* was actually watching her. She was reflecting on the contents of yesterday evening. She learned that her sister had unknowingly acquainted herself with the mother of her husband's child. Kara, or Rah, had explained that she wanted to separate herself from her past after her father died about six months back, and she'd legally changed her name to Rah Evans. According to Rah, she lived a simple life, under the radar, because she did not want anyone from her old life to find her. As far as she was concerned, that chapter of her life was closed.

Rah wanted to hear all the updates Investigator Anderson had on John. She demanded to know whether they were actually investigating in conjunction with the Person County Sheriff's Department. Danita observed how Rah really pressed Investigator Anderson; she even got into her face. In return, Investigator Anderson became political in her responses. Rah's presentation did not deter Investigator Anderson from questioning Rah rigorously and, in turn, getting in her face. She asked Rah what she had to hide and if she was hiding John. Danita recalled feeling the situation was going to spiral; however, Amir intervened. It was something about Rah that seemed off, but she figured it was her maternal instinct and being worried about her child.

This is ABC News. We interrupt your regularly scheduled program to bring you breaking news coverage. Authorities are reporting that the FC Attacker struck again last night, and we are being told there were two victims. All of the previous victims have been in Wake County; however, these two victims were in Edgecombe County. Despite the change in geographical location, authorities believe that it is indeed the FC Attacker. The authorities in Edgecombe County had an eyewitness to come forward in addition to other evidence found at the scenes. Wake & Edgecombe County officials believe that this is the break they needed to bring this assailant to justice. Stay tuned to ABC for more news updates. Now back to your regularly scheduled program.

Danita was stunned by the news interruption. There had not been any reported attacks in over a month. She was hoping that the police would conduct a thorough investigation and find the true culprit this time. She decided to call Diyah, who was on her way down, because her debit card had fallen out of her purse at their home the night before. She wanted to see if she had heard the news. She picked up her cell phone, found her contact, and waited for her to answer.

"Hey Danita, wassup? Did you need me to stop anywhere before I get there?" She asked, assuming that's why Danita was calling.

"No, actually, I was seeing if you'd heard the news?"

"What news, because I don't know if I can handle any more."

"The breaking news. The FC Attacker struck again. There were two victims this time. Seems like he's escalating."

"What!!!! No, I hadn't heard. What else did the news say?"

"They have an eyewitness, and apparently some other evidence was found at the scenes."

"That's good. I hope they get the right person this time, and justice will be served for all victims."

"Me too. It's definitely breaking news because they interrupted *The View*. How close are you to being here?"

"I just hit Spring Hope, so maybe about twelve minutes."

"Ok, I'll see you when you get here, and we'll replay it. Ma is beeping in."

"Ok, tell her I said hi and it wasn't me."

Danita laughed. "Ok," and she switched calls. Danita was on the phone with mom for about five minutes. They were discussing the news broadcast. Daisy was worried about how this might affect Diyah and whether people would think it was her who struck again. Daisy had not disclosed to anyone that she had gone to see Miguel last night, but she wondered if he, too, was one of the people who thought Diyah was behind last night's attacks. As Danita and Daisy were discussing their thoughts, the doorbell rang. "Hold on, ma, someone's at the door, and I don't think Diyah's gotten here that quickly." Danita got up and began walking towards the door. She saw through the fiberglass that it was Rah. *What is she doing here?* She thought to herself. "Ma, let me call you back. It's Rah."

"What is she doing there?" Daisy asked. Danita had filled Daisy in on everything late last night.

"I don't know, but I'm about to find out."

"Ok, call me back."

"Will do." Danita opened the door, but didn't invite Rah in. Rah was wearing a cream hoodie with matching pants and a pair of off white and brown gum Adidas. "Hey, Rah, this is unexpected. What are you doing here?"

"Hey, I'm sorry to pop up like this, but I didn't have y'all's number to call. I was hoping to speak with Amir privately if you don't mind."

"I mind," Amir responded. He had walked up on the tail end of their exchange. He was wearing a V-neck navy blue T-shirt, navy blue windbreaker pants, and black ankle socks.

"Hey Amir," Rah greeted him. "I had something private to discuss that might impact John," she explained.

"Anything you have to say can be said in front of my wife. So if you still want to share, come on in," he offered by opening the door wider. Danita stepped to the side so Rah could come in.

Rah came in and laughed nervously. "Again, I apologize for popping up," she said, looking at Danita and Amir. Then she looked around. They were still standing in the foyer. "I didn't get a chance to tell y'all last night, but you two have a lovely home."

"So what do you have to share that will impact John?" Amir got straight to the point, ignoring Rah's small talk. He knew Danita probably felt disrespected by Rah's spontaneous visit.

Rah hesitated for a few seconds. She began wringing her hands. "Well, I was hoping to ask for a favor?"

"What kind of favor?" Amir asked.

"I," Rah took a deep breath, looked down towards the floor, and shifted her weight from her right foot to her left. "I think I may need an alibi."

"Excuse me?" Danita asked before Amir had a chance to respond.

"I think I need an alibi," Rah repeated.

"Rah, I don't know what you've gotten yourself into, but it has nothing to do with me. How does this even relate to John?" Amir asked. He folded his arms.

"Well, if I go to jail, I won't be able to see him when he's found," Rah explained.

"I'm not following," Amir stated.

"I don't want the first time seeing my son to be a visitation while I'm locked up," Rah elaborated.

"What did you do?" Amir asked.

"Don't answer that," Danita interjected. "We don't want to know. My husband isn't going to lie for you, Rah. I'm sorry."

"Amir, think about John. He left his home to find us. I don't know what has happened to him. Do you really think seeing me in jail for the first time would be good for him?" Rah appealed to Amir. "Don't you think he's been through enough?" Amir became silent.

"Bae, you're not really considering this, are you?" Danita asked.

"I am considering how it will impact John," he said, looking at

156

Danita. He turned towards Rah and said, "But I'm not willing to lie for you despite how it'll impact him."

"Y'all owe me," Rah said.

"What?" Danita was perplexed.

"It's just," Rah paused. "Well, to be frank, I'm the reason your sister got out of jail," she explained.

"Ok, I've had enough of this. I think it's best you leave," Danita stated.

"Yeah, I agree, Kara, I mean Rah. I'm going to have to ask you to leave," Amir supported Danita.

"Not until you hear me out, please," Rah asked. Danita and Amir looked at one another. She took their silence as permission. She took another deep breath. "I'm the FC Attacker. When I learned that Diyah was arrested and they suspected her of being the FC Attacker, I attacked someone to create reasonable doubt for her," Rah admitted.

"Wait, so you're telling me you're the one who attacked her biological father?" Danita asked slowly, pointing at Rah while she spoke.

"Yes," Rah admitted.

"Then you're the reason she was locked up in the first place," Danita yelled. Amir pulled her back.

"I am, but I thought I was doing her a favor. I didn't mean for her to get caught up in it," Rah pleaded. "I'm sorry. I know I don't deserve it, but I'm asking that y'all reconsider my favor. I'm worried about this eyewitness report and the evidence left at the scenes. It could come back to me."

"You're crazy," Danita belittled her. Her nostrils were flared, and her heart was beating fast. "Wait until Diyah gets here."

"She's on her way here?" Rah's voice cracked.

"She'll be here any minute," Danita smiled.

"Let's just calm down," Amir finally spoke. "Let's try to think rationally."

"Oh, so you want me to calm down and think rationally?" Danita questioned Amir. "Do you hear what she's saying?" She was pointing at Rah again.

Amir took Danita's hands into his. He looked into her eyes and lowered his voice, "I do. I know this is a shock and it's upsetting, but I don't want anyone to do anything they'll later regret," he explained.

Danita pressed her lips together and nodded her head in agreement. She didn't like it, but she understood what Amir was saying. *Ding dong.* Everyone turned to the door.

"Oh God, that's Diyah," Rah said.

Danita glanced at Rah and walked over to the door to let Diyah in. She was wearing a navy blue plain hoodie, a long-sleeved white T-shirt, wide leg track pants with white stripes down the sides, and her white Adidas. Diyah took one look at Danita and then scanned the room. "What's going on? Rah, why are you here at my sister and brother-in-law's house?" Diyah then looked back at Danita, "You good, sis?"

"Everyone's fine," Amir answered. "Why don't everyone come into the living room so we can have a seat?"

"Nah, I want to know what's going on right now?" Diyah demanded. "Why is my sister upset?"

"Let's go to the living room like Amir suggested," Danita chimed in. She was trying to support Amir. She grabbed Diyah's hand and patted it. "Then Rah can explain everything."

Everyone walked towards the living room. Amir leading the way, Rah behind him, Danita and Diyah in the rear. Rah sat at one end of the sectional, and Diyah sat at the other, but she was on the edge of her seat. She removed her hoodie to give her agile capability if needed. Amir and Danita were in the middle, serving as barriers, just in case. Once everyone was seated, Diyah asked, "So, Rah, what's going on? What's all this about?" Rah explained to Diyah why she was there; she revealed that she was the FC Attacker. She also revealed that she was the one who attacked Miguel, and then, once learning that Diyah was arrested, she attacked someone else to help her case.

Diyah jumped up, "You what!!!!" Rah remained seated. Amir and Danita jumped up, too, in case they needed to intervene.

"Listen D," Rah said, trying to take control.

"Don't call me D," Diyah demanded.

"Fine, Diyah. I didn't mean for any of this to happen. I told you to get rid of those clothes. I told you to walk away."

"You're blaming me?" Diyah asked, taking a step towards Rah. She felt her heart racing.

"No, I'm just saying that I didn't think any of this would come back on you. I thought you would have taken my advice."

"Rah, you have some nerve. Why would you even come to see me after my release when you were the reason I was locked up? That was cold-blooded, and you know how I can get down," Diyah hissed through her teeth. She looked Rah up and down.

Rah stood up. "And now that you know I'm the FC Attacker, you know how I get down," she countered, taking a step forward.

"You attack old men from behind when they least expect it. I'm not them," Diyah stated matter-of-factly.

"I see that jailhouse religion wasn't real," Rah said sarcastically.

"Oh, it is real. That is about the only reason I haven't dragged you out of here," Diyah defended.

"Diyah, we all know how you *used to* get down," Danita intervened, stepping in the middle of them. "I know you're angry. Trust me, I understand. I'm angry too." She glared at Rah. "But remember, you're not the person you were once before. You're a new creature now. Do you want to be in your own will, in your feelings? Or do you want to be in God's perfect will?"

Diyah became silent. She began to process what Danita was saying. The last time she was led by her emotions, it led to an unwanted outcome.

"Can y'all just hear me out? Let me explain how this all started," Rah asked. "Maybe then you'll understand my actions and why I don't want to be locked up when I first meet John. Pleeease." Everyone looked at one another.

"Let's hear her out," Amir requested. He truly just wanted to keep everyone calm because he knew his wife and sister-in-law had a breaking point. Danita looked at Diyah; they were silently communicating with each other.

"Fine," Diyah said.

"Ok," Danita agreed too. Everyone sat down.

"Thank you," Rah took a deep breath. "You should know that I didn't have the ideal childhood. I wasn't beaten or sexually abused, nothing like that, but I was mentally abused by my mother. She constantly critiqued me. Nothing I did was ever good enough. My grades weren't high enough, even if I made straight A's. If I came home dirty from playing, she would scold me. 'Girls should always remain neat and clean,' she would say. I had to constantly watch what I ate. 'Girls should always have a small frame'. When I hit puberty, I naturally started to fill out. She put me on a strict diet. A size 10 was too big in her opinion. I always did what she asked. I so desperately wanted to please her. I just wanted her to truly be proud of me, just once. My father allowed my mom to have her way and treat me like she did most of the time, but if he spoke up, my mother respected what he said. She would say, 'a woman must always keep her man happy'. She was sick in the head, but I didn't realize that then. I was brainwashed by her philosophies. Then, I met Amir. Everything changed. My desire shifted from wanting to please my mom to wanting to spend time with him, breathe the air he breathed. I wanted to please him. My mom tried to get me back under her control, but it didn't work. My father encouraged my mother to allow me to date. I was of age, he said, so my mother respected my father's wishes, of course. We were madly in love, and that's what led to the pregnancy," Rah paused and looked at Danita. "I'm sorry."

Danita cleared her throat, "It's ok, go ahead."

"My mom blamed my dad for my getting pregnant. I caused shame to the family. She made it seem like I was the first teenage girl to get pregnant ever. She demanded that I place the child for adoption. I didn't want to. She told me that if I didn't, they would kick me out, and I would be on my own with a newborn. She told me that eventually the child would be taken because I wouldn't be able to take care of it without support. My mother was so manipulative. I went to my father for his help. He encouraged me to place the child for adoption, too. He said I was too young and I had my whole life ahead of me. I didn't have any support. I was scared into agreement."

"Kara, why didn't you tell me any of this?" Amir asked.

"Rah, she corrected him."

"Rah, what didn't you tell me any of this?" He repeated. "I would have supported you."

Rah began to tear up. "She convinced me that you were just a boy yourself and you would leave me. It wasn't hard to believe. How many other girls did we see that happen to in our high school? Anyways, my mom convinced your parents that adoption was best for us. I admired you, Amir. You stood up to your parents."

"I eventually gave in," Amir expressed with guilt.

Rah wiped tears from her face. "You put up a good fight. I understood why you did. All of us were pressuring you." She paused before continuing. "Anyways, my mom died 3 years ago. Colon cancer. Dad and I took care of her until the end. She suffered, and I'm thankful she did. She was the cancer if you asked me. Then, 2 years later, dad got sick. He was diagnosed with prostate cancer. I took care of him. He knew he was dying near the end. He apologized to me and confessed that he was wrong for not standing up to my mom all those years. He said that he figured a mother knew best for her daughter. He apologized for the adoption. He said that he didn't stop the adoption because he supported it 100% and it was his idea. He asked for my forgiveness, but I didn't give it to him. All that time, I thought it was my mom's idea. When he finally died, I handled his affairs, settled the estate, sold the house, changed my name from Kara Dakota Finch to Rah Dakota Evans, and relocated to the city. I was done with my old life. My family knew how my mom was, and no one intervened. I wanted to be free, to party every day. Live life on my terms. I didn't plan on becoming the *FC Attacker*. One night, I was out, and I saw a daughter and her father arguing. I saw myself in her. I saw her pain, her hurt, I felt her sadness. Once she left, I followed her dad, and before I knew it, I attacked him because I saw my father in him. I was shocked. It was like someone else was in control, but it felt good. I felt alive. Then, I would plan who to attack, and it just kept happening." Rah looked straight ahead towards Diyah. "When you told me about your biological father and your plan was discovered, I thought it was divine intervention. Unbeknownst to you, you were talking to the FC Attacker. I didn't want you to go down my path, but I wanted to fulfill your desire, as well as my own. I never wanted you to get charged for his attack or any of the attacks. That's why I tried to help you out, throwing the police off while you were locked up. Then I told myself I'd quit if you got out, and I did, but then I learned about John and his disappearance. That caused me to relapse. It's all my dad's fault that all of this happened. None of this would have happened had John been raised by us. I went back to Tarboro for the first time, and all of the memories came flooding back." Rah paused to steady her breath. She looked at everyone, but her eyes settled on Amir last. "I just hope my baby boy is ok. And when he shows up, I want to hold him in my arms, I want to smell his hair. I don't want to meet him for the first time being locked up."

Amir didn't respond.

"So, you expect to never pay for what you've done?" Danita asked.

"No, not at all. I'll turn myself in. I just need 48 hours from the time he surfaces."

"We don't know when that will be?" Danita highlighted. "I hope John shows up any day now, but technically, we don't know when. What are you going to do in the meantime? Go on attacking fathers like you did last night?

"No," Rah stated firmly.

"How do you know that? Once you're triggered, that's it," Danita pressed.

"Had I not been sloppy last night, I probably would have continued on attacking, but now my freedom is more important to me. My desire to be free, to meet my son, is greater than my displaced sense of revenge. Unfortunately, my son will find out about my actions, and I want to set a good example by taking ownership. If y'all can just help me avoid arrest. I feel any evidence will be circumstantial, but I may need an alibi if the police come knocking at my door." Everyone sat silently, each in their own respective thoughts.

"Rah, I'm sorry about your childhood. I'm sorry you didn't have supportive, loving parents. I understand you a little better now, but it still hurts me that you attacked Miguel, and I was arrested for your actions," Diyah expressed. Her tone had softened. "I understand that I told you I wanted him to be attacked and I was planning to do it, but I can't say for sure that I would have followed through. When I confronted him that night, I could have attacked him then, openly, but I didn't, despite my fury. He hurt me, but I didn't want to do him bodily harm. He is my father after all."

"I understand. If I could turn back the hands of time, I would. I'm sorry again, Diyah. I really am," Rah expressed her regret.

"I believe you. It's gonna take me some time to forgive you, though, but I know I will," Diyah responded.

"Thanks, I don't deserve your compassion," Rah said, sobbing in full-blown tears. Danita gave her some Kleenex. Once she calmed down, she asked, "So will y'all help me if I need it? I don't have anyone else to ask that I can trust."

Danita looked at Diyah and Amir. "I don't want no parts of this. I feel for her, I really do, but I think y'all should think rationally."

Danita looked directly at Amir as she said, rationally, using his words against him.

"I don't think I would be a solid alibi if I wanted to be, considering my integrity is being questioned," Diyah highlighted.

"True, I get that," Rah said. "Amir? How about you? Think about our son."

"I have thought about him. I've also been thinking about what kind of father I want to be. I hope you can avoid the authorities long enough until John is found, but you definitely should turn yourself in."

"I will, in 48 hours of his return. I promise," Rah reiterated.

"That's good to hear. With that being said, I can't provide an alibi. I want to be the kind of father who honors the Lord above everyone," he explained.

Rah wiped a few more tears from her eyes. "Ok, well, thanks for hearing me out. I don't have any other reason to be here, so I'll leave. Would you keep me posted on John if you hear anything?" She asked Amir as she stood up.

"Of course," Amir agreed. He stood up too. "You take care of yourself, Rah, and please try to control yourself. I'll be praying for your peace."

"Thanks." She turned towards Danita, "Thank you for allowing me into your home."

"Mmmmm-hm," all she could do was acknowledge Rah's gratitude. She remained seated.

"Take care of yourself, Diyah," Rah bid her farewell.

"You too, Rah," Diyah expressed.

Rah turned to walk to the door. "I'll walk you to the door," Amir offered. As they were walking to the door, they saw someone through the fiberglass. *Ding. Dong.*

"Who's that?" Danita called out.

"I don't know, whoever has their back to the door. They're wearing a black hoodie." Amir called back. He reached the door, opened it, and said, "Can I help you?" The person turned around, and they locked eyes. Amir felt like he was looking in a mirror and seeing his teenage self. "John?" He whispered. He felt like he was dreaming.

He extended his hand, "It's nice to meet you, sir. I'm JJ."

Chapter 20
Family Reunion

Amir's mouth was slightly open. His eyes widened, and then he blinked several times to make sure his eyes were not deceiving him. JJ was slightly shorter than Amir; he was about 6'2", slim, muscular build, tawny brown complexion like his mother, and he had a low taper fade. He was wearing a black hoodie, black jeans, and a pair of red/black/gray Jordans. "Sir?" JJ repeated. "You are Amir Franklin, correct?"

Amir snapped out of his shock. "Yes, I am Amir, your birth father. I've been waiting 16 years to meet you, John," Amir shook JJ's hand. He observed his firm handshake. "I've imagined this day so many times. The pleasure is all mine. Do you mind if I hug you?" Amir asked. His voice cracked.

"No, sir, I don't mind," JJ smiled and consented.

"It's John, y'all!" Rah shouted with joy to notify Danita and Diyah.

Amir hugged JJ for about 20 seconds. He didn't want to let go, but he felt that if he'd hugged him any longer, he might cause JJ to feel awkward. After releasing him, he said, "Please come on in. This is your birth mom." Amir was pointing to Rah. He noticed that Danita and Diyah were observing at the end of the hall. He assumed they hung back to give them their moment.

Rah was crying uncontrollably as she hugged JJ and rubbed his back. "I can't believe it's you. I can't believe you're here," she kept repeating. After about a minute, Rah released JJ but held his hand. She stepped back and said to JJ, "Let me take a look at you." After a few seconds of taking him in, she turned to Amir and asked, "I know I was getting ready to go, but do you mind if I stay?"

Amir looked up at Danita, who, along with Diyah, were now in tears. She mouthed "of course" to Amir. "Yes, absolutely," he assured Rah. "Why don't we all transition to the living room?" He suggested. As they neared Danita and Diyah, Amir made introductions.

"John, it's a pleasure to meet you. Would you like anything to drink or eat?" Danita asked. She was wondering when the last time he might've eaten, since no one knew where he'd been.

"I'm good right now, thank you," he responded.

"Ok, well, let me know if you change your mind," Danita turned towards Amir. She reached for his hand, "I'm going to give you three the living room to have some privacy, ok?

"Ok, thanks, babe. You're the best," Amir squeezed and kissed Danita's hands.

"I'll head on out. I'll check in on y'all later," Diyah bid her farewell. She didn't try to interrupt Rah, who had begun to engage John in small talk on the couch. She was happy that Amir, Rah, and John had reconnected. She knew how it felt to have that void. Seeing Rah with John provoked compassion, and in that moment, she decided to forgive her. Danita walked Diyah to the door, they hugged, and Danita exited to her bedroom.

For the next hour, Amir, Rah, and JJ were getting to know one another. He asked if he could call them Amir and Rah vs Mr. Franklin and Ms. Evans. JJ expressed that he would like to be called JJ because John seemed too formal for his age. He'd also informed them that his parents named him John because the disciple John had a close connection with Jesus, so much so that Jesus entrusted Mary's care to John during the crucifixion. Per JJ, his parents showed him in the book of John from the Bible, that John often described himself as "the disciple whom Jesus loved." Per JJ, his parents wanted him to know he had a special place in their hearts because he was loved dearly. JJ learned about Amir and Rah's careers, he learned about his deceased maternal grandparents' deaths, and that he had living paternal grandparents and an uncle.

Amir and Rah learned that after JJ left his home, he initially planned to find them right away, but he admitted he was nervous and delayed contact until after Christmas. He explained that his parents did not know an old friend was back in his life. JJ further explained that after Christmas, he borrowed his friend's car and sought out Rah first, but he had no luck until he came to Amir's last night and overheard the exchange with them outside.

"Once I learned that the Investigator was inside, I decided to come back today. I knew the police would want to take over and ask questions, but I wanted my time. I had questions of my own," JJ explained.

"What questions do you have?" Amir asked.

"I want to know why y'all decided to place me in adoption. I don't blame you, but I do want to know. I want to hear it from you," he asked.

"My parents felt like it was the best decision considering how young Amir and I were. I didn't want to place you in adoption, and neither did Amir. I eventually gave in because I was led to believe I would be on my own, with a newborn, and no support. I didn't want that for you," Rah explained. "I was convinced your father wouldn't have helped me, but I didn't realize until later that it was a lie. Amir and his parents would have helped."

"My parents also believed that adoption was best, considering our ages, like Rah said. I knew it would be hard, but I wanted to try-"

"Amir was pressured by all of us; he really held out until the end before consenting," Rah interrupted Amir. She didn't want JJ blaming Amir. "And we all participated in selecting your parents. We chose not to know your sex because we felt like it would have been harder to follow through the more we knew about you."

"I understand. I can't imagine having a child at this age, let alone trying to raise it," JJ empathized.

"We want you to know that you were wanted, JJ. The timing was just off. Placing you in adoption was one of the hardest decisions of my life, and equally, it's a decision I regret the most," Amir expressed.

"My parents treat me well. I love them and they love me. Y'all chose well," JJ expressed with gratitude.

"That's good to hear," Rah let out a sigh of relief. "I'm curious, what made them tell you that you were adopted now?"

"I was getting suspicious. It started about a year ago. I didn't think I was adopted, but I knew they were hiding something. There were signs over a period of time. I had to get a new pediatrician because my old one closed their practice. I asked if I could go back alone at my initial appointment with my new pediatrician. My mom told me I could, but she had to go back privately first, in case the doctor had any questions I couldn't answer. I didn't understand why she had to go back privately, and I felt like she was hiding something. Then there were other signs. I have a little sister, she's five years younger. My mom gave birth to her. I remember her being pregnant. Her name is Johanna. I guess she was feeling nostalgic one day and went through old photos. She found pictures from our mom's maternity shoot and her gender reveal. I didn't think nothing of it, but Johanna asked where the pictures were of when mom was pregnant with me and my gender reveal. I could tell my parents were caught off guard. They said that since I was their first child, they didn't want to jinx anything bad happening, so they played it safe. I didn't buy it. I felt like they were lying. Finally, I learned about blood types in biology. One day, when I went in for a routine wellness exam, I asked my pediatrician to identify my blood type since she had to draw labs. I learned through MyChart that I'm type O. I asked my parents their blood type without them knowing that I had gotten my blood type. My father is type B, and my mother is type AB. I questioned how I could be type O. They brushed it off and said my lab test must've been an error. They told me not to worry about it, and if I ever needed blood, I'd get the right blood type then. I kept pressing them. I knew something was off. Finally, they told me shortly after my 16th birthday. I was more hurt by their secrecy than I was by finding out that I was adopted. I wanted to meet y'all for obvious reasons, and I couldn't trust that what they were telling me was true, considering they'd already lied to me. So here I am."

"I see," Rah commented. "Well, my blood type is O, like yours."

"And, I'm type B," Amir offered.

"That makes more sense," JJ chuckled.

"You know, JJ, I've been enjoying our personal time, but we might need to call your parents. Rah and I have been worried, so I know they have. We probably need to call Investigator Anderston, too, now that I think of it," Amir suggested.

"No, not yet. My parents are just going to take me home. I'm not ready to leave."

"We're not ready for you to go," Rah pulled JJ into her arms.

"No, we're not, but it's only right to call," Amir encouraged.

"*I need this time,*" Rah looked at Amir, and she continued to hold JJ. She was hoping he understood what she meant. She didn't want to waste her 48 hours.

Amir knew what Rah was saying. Truthfully, he didn't want JJ's parents to take him home yet either. "JJ, do you think your parents would be open to staying here with you for a few days. We have enough space. That way, you could also meet my parents and my brother."

"That's a great idea. I'd love that. I don't know how they'd feel about it, but I can explain that I'm not ready to leave and I hope to keep in contact after I go home."

"I'd love to keep in contact," Amir expressed.

"Me too," Rah said. She felt an ache in her heart. She knew that if JJ and his parents were open to it, their communication would be different with her incarceration. She hated what she'd become. She never imagined that her decisions would interfere with her relationship with her child. "Amir, do you think you and Danita would be ok with me staying here too if his parents agree?"

"I'd have to discuss it with Danita," Amir stated.

"I hope we all can be here together," JJ expressed. "I do miss my parents and Johanna." He turned to Rah. "Why'd you change your name? And what's the significance of Evans?"

"Evans was my maternal grandmother's maiden name. She was a strong woman. How about I explain the rest while Amir calls your parents and Investigator Anderson," Rah suggested. Amir got JJ's parents' numbers from him. Then he headed to the bedroom because he wanted to talk to Danita first about Rah, JJ, and his parents staying over until Friday. Fifteen minutes later, Amir returned to the living room.

"What did Danita and JJ's parents say?" Rah asked with desperation.

"*Everyone* thinks it's a great idea that we spend a couple of days together. JJ, your parents actually want to speak with you," Amir handed JJ his cell phone. JJ took the phone from Amir, and Amir motioned for Rah to follow him into the kitchen. "So, Danita is going to get the guest bedrooms ready. Once JJ gets off the phone, we can get an idea of things to buy because we're going to need groceries to accommodate everyone for a couple of days."

"This is so exciting. Thank you, Amir. I will thank Danita personally if that's ok. This means so much to me."

"I know it does. I'm excited myself. God answered our prayers. He was safe the entire time. I can't wait for my parents and Isaiah to meet him."

"It'll be good seeing your parents and Isaiah, too. I probably need to run home and pack a bag. I hate to leave, but I don't want to be walking around in the same outfit for days."

"Danita has extra toiletries. Why don't you run to Walmart and buy a change of clothes to save time and gas?"

"That's a great idea. I'll wait until we make the grocery list. Maybe Danita and I can go together?"

"I'm sure she'll be fine with that."

Investigator Anderson came to meet JJ and asked him a few questions privately. She spoke with the Jacobson's and they confirmed with Investigator Anderson that she could leave him in the care of his birth parents. Two and a half hours later, Danita and

Rah had just finished cooking JJ's favorite: fried chicken, cream potatoes, and green peas, just as JJ's parents and Johanna had arrived.

Introductions were made. JJ's father was Morris Jacobson. He was 45 years old, had a medium brown complexion, stood 6'2", and was wearing a brown polo, tinted jeans, and brown duck boots. Come here, JJ, we've missed you, son," he said, giving JJ a bear hug.

"I missed you, too, dad," JJ responded.

Diane Jacboson was JJ's mother. She was 43 years old, had a medium brown complexion, stood 5'6", and was wearing a brown sweater, tinted skinny jeans, and brown Hey Dudes. She hugged JJ next. "Thank God for your safety. We're sorry, JJ," she expressed. She was crying. After she and JJ broke away, he looked over to Johanna. She was an 11-year-old, medium brown complexion, stood 4'9", wore clear rectangle eye glasses, and was wearing a green, pink, and yellow sweater with jean overalls, and pink crocs.

"Don't I get a hug?" He asked. She didn't respond. "You mad at me?"

"You had us all worried, JJ," Johanna admitted.

"I know. I'm sorry. I won't do something like this again. I missed you, though. Can I please get a hug?" Johanna happily gave in and hugged her big brother.

"I miss you too, JJ," she expressed. After she finished hugging JJ, she asked, "What did you do to your hair?" She was referencing the absence of his double-strand twists.

"I cut my hair. I knew the police were looking for a teen to fit my description. I figured cutting my hair would give me a disguise and buy me time to find my birth parents."

"I don't like it," Johanna commented. Everyone laughed.

After dinner was done, William, Belle, and Isaiah showed up to join everyone for dessert, German chocolate cake, another one of JJ's favorites. Amir had suggested they arrive a little later than the Jacobsons, so they could give the Jacobsons some time to reconnect with JJ first. Belle ran to JJ first, introduced herself, and hugged him tightly. She was wearing a royal purple sweater, vintage jeans, and a black pair of Clarks. Next, William introduced himself. He shook JJ's hand. He was wearing a royal blue sweater, dark denim jeans, and his brown leather shoes. Lastly, Isaiah introduced himself to his nephew, and he dapped him up. He was wearing a black Nike fleece wind runner, black windbreaker pants, black socks, and black Crocs. Amir introduced the rest of the Jacobsons to his family. Belle sat down with everyone at the dining table. William and Isaiah had to sit at the island to have dessert because there was no more room at the dining room table. The families continued talking and getting to know one another, laughing, and taking pictures well into the night.

Ding. Dong. It was Thursday, December 28th, and Diyah stood outside of Danita and Amir's door. She called Rah late last night, asking to come over today to talk briefly. Rah agreed. Diyah decided to door dash and come over later in the evening to not interrupt Rah's time with JJ. Diyah was wearing a jean jacket, over a gray sweater, black leggings, and her old, solid black UGG boots.

"Hey sis, come on in," Danita greeted her. She was wearing a black round-neck knitted loungewear set and her black bedroom shoes. "How are you doing? I didn't get a chance to call you last night. I was exhausted."

"I'm sure you were. You are in full-blown hostess mode," Diyah acknowledged.

"I am in hostess mode. I can't stop yawning, although I slept well last night. I'm ready for bed now. But you still didn't tell me how you were, you know, with finding out about Rah's secret activity," Danita inquired.

"Initially, it was a shock, and I was furious. You know that."

"Yeah, yeah. I knew you were, and I was livid too."

"But seeing her with John-"

"JJ, he prefers to be called JJ."

"Oh, well, seeing her with JJ provoked compassion for her even more after hearing her story. Her parents were horrible."

"Shh, not too loud. I don't want her to hear you."

"Anyways, I decided to forgive her before I left here yesterday. I'm good. How's Amir? You?"

"We're thankful, happy, blessed," Danita said with a big smile. "It brings me so much joy to see how happy Amir is."

"I'm happy for him, Rah, and JJ too. I really am," Diyah smiled back at Danita. "Anyways, I'm ready to get on back home, so where's Rah?"

"She's upstairs. I put an electric heater in the garage to warm it up for you two. Y'all will have the most privacy there since all the bedrooms upstairs are near one another. I'll go up and get her."

"Thanks. Listen, I'll let myself out. Go on and start getting ready for bed," Diyah reached to hug Danita. "Good night, sis."

"Good night. Text me that you made it home safely. I love you," Danita began to climb the steps to let Rah know that Diyah was downstairs in the garage.

"I love you too," Diyah said as she was leaving for the garage.

Three minutes later, Rah was entering the garage. She was wearing a black pajama set with moons and stars all over, and a black satin bonnet. "Hey Diyah, what's going on?"

"Hey, Rah, how are you doing? Are you and JJ connecting?"

"Yes, I think we are. He's such a smart, respectful kid with plans to go to college; he's perfect. I'm on cloud 9," Rah paused. Her smile faded. "But I know you didn't drive all the way to Nashville to ask about JJ and I. What's up?"

"Are you still planning on turning yourself in tomorrow?"

"Is that why you drove out here?"

"Not exactly, but are you?"

"Yes, I am. I'm dreading it desperately, though, but it'll be better for me to turn myself in than to have them arrest me. I haven't told JJ anything yet. I'm going to tell him tomorrow.

I was afraid that if I mentioned it sooner, he'd share with his parents, and my time with him would be cut short."

"Yeah, I understand all of that."

"You still haven't told me why you drove out here to see me?"

"I remember how lonely I felt in jail. I mean, my family came to my rescue, but they didn't understand what I was going through. I know I only spent 8 days on the inside, but I have perspective. You don't have anyone to come see you, I mean, hopefully JJ will, but you don't know. I want to be your support if you'd allow me to be?"

"Are you serious? You want to support me, the person who is responsible for your 8-day vacation?"

"I know, it sounds crazy, but I do. I've forgiven you. And, pending you're not too far away, I'd visit, write, and drop some money in your commissary account when I could. I just want to keep you encouraged while you're in there, and pray over you."

"This doesn't make sense. Why would you do this for me?"

"Our stories are different, but they have great similarities, Rah. We were both hurt by our parents, and that hurt turned into anger and stupid decisions. We both have been fools. Well, let me call myself a fool. I was heading down a one-way street and going the wrong way. But my family didn't turn their backs on me. I want to pay it forward, considering you don't have any support. Would you feel comfortable with that?"

Rah pondered for a few seconds. "If you're really serious?"

"I am."

"Then, I'd greatly appreciate it. I would like to add you to my accounts and as a beneficiary."

"Wait. What?"

"Diyah, I'm not expecting the worst, but I want to prepare for it. Death could happen. Besides, I want you to have access to my account in case JJ needs something."

"Rah, he has the Jacobsons."

"I know. But now that I can, I want to gift him birthday and Christmas gifts, at a minimum, if his parents will allow me. Can I meet you in Knightdale in the morning so we can go to my bank?"

"You're going to trust me with your money?"

"Should I not?"

"I'm not a thief, but you don't know that."

"I don't have much choice, you know. Besides, I can tell that your jailhouse religion is for real. I know the old Diyah, and you were supposed to jump on me like white on rice, but you didn't, and now…now you're offering to support me during my time. I-I don't deserve your kindness."

"That's how we should feel about God, because of His love, He shows us mercy, undeserved kindness and compassion. The Bible tells me that since I am His child, I must be an imitator of Him and walk in the way of love. He loves you, Rah."

"Here you go with your religious talk."

"I'm just saying, you know. He does. You're going to need Him in there. I didn't rededicate my life until the last day, and I didn't know it was my last day. Once I rededicated my life, I had peace. I was still locked up, I had no knowledge that I was getting out, but I had peace. Those 7 days prior were hell."

"I hear you. Thanks for offering your support, Diyah. So, can we go to my bank in the morning?"

"You're welcome. Yes, we can, but with this new information, I'll be adding some of your own money to your commissary. I am indebted to my family. I gotta reimburse them my lawyer fees."

That's fine," Rah gave a small laugh. "So I'll meet you at the Wells Fargo in Knightdale at 9 AM tomorrow morning."

"Ok, sounds like a plan. Anything else?"

Rah paused. "I'm scared, Diyah," Rah began to tear up.

"I understand, I do. If you let Him, He'll be right there with you. You have nothing to lose, but everything to gain by repenting and accepting Him."

Rah began to cry. "I need to get myself together first."

Diyah laughed. "Honey, it takes His blood to clean us up. If we could do it ourselves, we would. His love paid it all."

"Do you think He'll help me get out of this mess I made?"

"You're going to have to pay for your crimes, but He will grant you protection and favor while you're going through. And, you have so much life ahead of you that He wants to bless as you live life for Him. I'm not pressuring you, but don't wait. As a matter of fact, you were the one a few minutes ago who said death can happen. Well, I would want to be saved before I die. To be honest, had I been saved and reading my Bible, I feel I'd've never gone to jail. I was led by my flesh and not His spirit."

"Yeah, I can relate to the latter." Rah wiped tears from her face. "I'm going to do it. I'm going to give my life to Him. Will you lead me? What do I say?"

Diyah clapped her hands together, "Hallelujah!" She grabbed Rah's hands. "Repeat after me, 'God, I confess that your son Jesus died for my sins and rose on the third day with all power in His hands. I confess that I am a sinner and I have sinned against you. I want to live the rest of my life serving you and building your Kingdom. I repent, I ask you to come into my heart and cleanse me with your blood. Jesus, I now confess that you are my Lord and Savior. I thank you, in your name, Amen.' " Rah repeated after Diyah after every so many words. Afterwards, Diyah gave Rah a heartfelt hug. Diyah was smiling, "Now you gotta tell someone that you're saved."

Rah wiped more tears from her eyes. "Diyah?"

"Yeah?"

"I'm saved!"

"Ha! I didn't mean me, but glory to God anyhow. The angels are rejoicing! You're a part of God's family now. Everything won't be easy, but He'll be right there, leading you and guiding you."

"I have so much to learn."

"He's a teacher, but I can request a study Bible be sent to you so you can read and study His word."

"Thanks, Diyah, for everything. I'm indebted to you."

"All to Him you owe, not me, but you're welcome, Rah. Listen, I'm getting ready to go. I'll see you at 9 in the morning. Good night."

"Ok, drive home safely. Good night, Diyah."

The next day, Diyah met Rah at Wells Fargo at 9 AM as planned. Diyah was added as a joint owner to all of Rah's accounts and was later changed to Rah's beneficiary. To Diyah's surprise, Rah was left a lump sum of money from her parents, and she still had most of the proceeds from selling their home. Diyah now understood why Rah never seemed to be stressed over money. Rah gave Diyah the keys to her apartment and asked her to pack up her apartment, put her items in storage, and turn in her keys to the landlord. Diyah prayed for Rah and gave her a supportive hug before they departed.

After Rah left Diyah, she returned to Amir and Danita's home to have a farewell lunch with JJ, Amir, his family, and the Jacobsons.

She shared with everyone that she accepted Jesus the night before, and everyone rejoiced. They ate tossed salad, lasagna, and garlic bread. Afterwards, the Jacobsons, including JJ, gathered their luggage so they could leave. Danita and Amir's family all loved on JJ before bidding him farewell. Everyone ensured that the connection would remain. Rah asked to speak with JJ and his parents privately as they walked outside. With Danita's encouragement, Amir joined them. Morris sensed this conversation did not need to include Johanna, so he sent her to the car to warm it up.

Rah disclosed to JJ and his parents that she was the FC Attacker, and she would turn herself in after they returned to Roxboro. Rah explained to JJ what led to her becoming the FC Attacker, and she admitted she knew her actions were wrong but was not thinking rationally. JJ cried, and Diane consoled him. After JJ calmed down, Rah apologized to him. She expressed that she hopes she and JJ can remain connected; however, she understood if he didn't want to or if his parents would not allow it. JJ verbalized that he would like to write her at a minimum. She gave JJ a nurturing hug with his consent. Lastly, Amir gave JJ a comforting hug and expressed his love for him.

JJ wiped tears from his face. "Rah, my mom taught me **Joshua 1:9** anytime I expressed to her that I had anxiety about going somewhere new. It states to be 'strong and courageous. Do not be afraid; do not be discouraged, for the Lord your God will be with you wherever you go.' Memorize that."

"I will, thanks, JJ." Morris motioned for JJ to come on to the car so they could leave. Diane followed.

Rah and Amir returned to Amir's home. Rah thanked both Amir and Danita for their compassion and hospitality. Rah asked to leave her clothes there for Diyah to pick up later because she was heading directly to the Wake County Police Department to turn herself in. Rah also asked Danita to help Amir look after JJ. Danita and Amir prayed for Rah and gave her hugs before she left. Rah turned towards their door to leave. She wasn't ready to become a prisoner to her fate, but she was hopeful because she had Diyah as a support and, more importantly, she had faith that the Lord her God was with her wherever she went.

The End

Epilogue

Thanksgiving morning. Diyah was sitting on her couch, in her living room, in her pumpkin pajamas, drinking a cup of green tea. Jaylen and Sierra were on each side of her. She was reflecting over the past two Thanksgivings. A year and a half ago, she learned that Dawson was not her biological father and Thanksgiving last year, she was incarcerated for a crime she did not commit. Her bondage had been replaced with freedom, and she was grateful. She was still living a life of love for God, and she joined a church in Raleigh, NC. She served as a greeter two Sundays out of the month. She had gotten a job as a nurse researcher in Raleigh making 6 figures a year. Despite the increase in her income, she decided to remain in the apartment, living below her means, so she could pay her parents back, and Danita and Amir.

Her relationship with Dawson had developed tremendously, and, to her surprise, Miguel had reached out at the beginning of the year to apologize. He also asked if they could get to know one another, and he would like to introduce her to his other two children. Diyah gladly accepted Miguel's apology and his invitation for them to connect. He welcomed her back to the gym, and he was teaching her how to box. She admired his boxing skill, and she got the sense that he showed off for her when he was sparring. She recognized that he was making a great effort to build their relationship. To add to her surprise, he even paid off her restitution debt. He checked in on her, included her in family outings, he honored her 30th birthday, and she would be celebrating Noche Buena with them on Christmas Eve. As she continued to reflect, she laughed at how much she had become like Danita, because now she was a big sister to her 21-year-old sister, Marisol, and 17-year-old brother, Adolfo. She was thankful that her relationship with her paternal biological family was growing.

Diyah smiled when she thought about Danita. She and Amir

welcomed their rainbow baby, a healthy baby girl, on September 24th. Her name was Angel Danielle Franklin. She weighed 7lbs, 1 ounce at birth. Angel was spoiled by her parents, grandparents, big brother JJ, Uncle Isaiah, and her Tía. Diyah was embracing her Hispanic origins, which was why she planned to teach Angel to call her Tía instead of Aunt. She didn't know what Dené would want Angel to call her, since she and Isaiah had become engaged on Valentine's Day earlier in the year. They planned to marry on February 15th in the new year. With the additions to the family: JJ, Angel, and Dené, Diyah was planning Christmas pictures for herself and her family. This time, she would also remember to include Jaylen and Sierra. She'd asked Miguel about them taking family pictures so she would also have pictures with him, his wife, and her paternal siblings. He agreed and asked Diyah to coordinate with his wife to plan the photoshoot.

Diyah smiled. She was proud of her inward transformation and in awe of the outpouring of God's blessings upon her life. She was also thankful that God was faithful to Rah as she served her time. She was sentenced to 7 years in prison. Diyah was keeping her word; she was praying over Rah, visiting her at Anson Correctional Institution once every 2 months, writing to her, and making sure her commissary account had money. JJ also kept his word, and he wrote to Rah once a month. They all hoped that Rah would be released sooner than 7 years for good behavior. She was a model inmate from their understanding, and she also was an inspiration to the other inmates, sharing the gospel of Jesus Christ. Diyah was thankful that God was using her and Rah's mess for His glory; after all, the most important purpose was to advance His Kingdom.

Meet the Author
Davneatra Foster Campbell

Scan me

Follow Me on Facebook

Davneatra Foster Campbell is a proud Nashville, North Carolina, native whose life is grounded in faith and purpose. A devoted wife and follower of Christ, she finds joy in every role she fulfills—daughter, sister, Auntie, cat mom, sorority sister, and now, the 2025 She Woke Up Scribe Award recipient.

With a bachelor's degree from Fayetteville State University and a Master of Social Work from the University of Southern California, Davneatra brings nearly two decades of experience as a licensed clinical social worker. Her work in mental health has deepened her compassion for people and strengthened her desire to write stories that heal the heart.

Encouraged by her mother's words that true writers have something meaningful to say, Davneatra found her inspiration in life itself. Through her fiction, she weaves faith, wisdom, and hope into narratives that encourage, motivate, and awaken transformation—reminding readers that even in the hardest seasons, grace still speaks.

Have you read?

If not, it is availible on amazon.com!

www.ingramcontent.com/pod-product-compliance
Lightning Source LLC
Chambersburg PA
CBHW070031120726
47909CB00003B/1119